Puffin Books
Editor: Kaye We...
The Midwinter ...

Charlotte opened the door cautiously and peered out.
(You can't be too careful!) On the doorstep stood a fat,
foreign-looking man. Japanese? Or Chinese? He wanted
Mischa Lewis, the violinist, who lived in the extension
to their house, but when Charlotte told him Mischa
wasn't there he didn't go away. She could see him
from the window, stalking up and down outside,
watching their house.

'He's like a big cat,' she told her brother. 'He's got a
fat round face and a bow round his neck. He's waiting
for the mouse.' She *said* that, but she wasn't scared of
the stranger yet. Not yet! Being scared came later, after
her parents went away and after her exams. Being
really scared came with the snow and the body they
found in Mischa's flat; it came with Mischa's
disappearance and the discovery that something very
dangerous and evil, another kind of snow that wasn't
so Christmassy, had been packed in the
innocent-looking case containing violins from Japan.

Darkness and cold, the shortest day and the longest
suspense, that was what Charlotte remembered later.
Would Mischa ever be found, and would Christmas, a
proper Christmas, ever come again, all peace and
happiness?

This very exciting thriller, with its lively characters
set in a sophisticated Chelsea background, is Sally
Bicknell's first novel for young people.

To Lynda —
hope you feel better!

Ricky Morgan
1977

Sally Bicknell

The Midwinter Violins

Puffin Books

Puffin Books,
Penguin Books Ltd,
Harmondsworth, Middlesex, England
Penguin Books,
625 Madison Avenue, New York,
New York 10022, U.S.A.
Penguin Books Australia Ltd,
Ringwood, Victoria, Australia
Penguin Books Canada Ltd,
41 Steelcase Road West, Markham, Ontario, Canada
Penguin Books (N.Z.) Ltd,
182–190 Wairau Road, Auckland 10, New Zealand

First published by Chatto & Windus 1973
Published in Puffin Books 1976
Copyright © Sally Bicknell, 1973

Made and printed in Great Britain by
Hazell Watson & Viney Ltd,
Aylesbury, Bucks
Set in Linotype Pilgrim

Contents

To Effie, with love

We Three Kings

I

'Don't work too hard, Charlotte,' said the parents. 'It's not the end of the world if you don't get in. You can always try again later.'

Kind and casual, wonderful parents. I was going to take university entrance exams at the end of the year. They pretended not to care whether I got in or not, but I knew they did really. And as for me, I cared desperately.

I remember taking my books everywhere with me that summer. I worked most of the time, in a dreadful frenzy. There was a family holiday in Scotland. I worked sitting on the beach, the smell of seaweed in my nose. I worked on the hillside, resting my books on springy heather. When it rained I took shelter in the boat-house and worked there. I worked in the cottage kitchen in the evenings, by the light of a hissing paraffin lamp. Then home to London, a few more days till school started again, and I settled gratefully back into my room on the top floor and went on working.

The house seemed hot and stuffy after cool, damp Scotland. Summer noises drifted in through the open window, buses in the King's Road, cars turning sharply in our square, distant voices and laughter. It was the last warm night before autumn and rain and falling leaves.

It must have been nearly eleven o'clock when the front doorbell rang. The parents were out. The Bowens, who lived in the basement, were asleep in bed. My stepbrother John, who was down on the ground floor watching television, could have done something about the insistent ringing, but he was obviously pretending not to hear. Typical. I left my desk and went downstairs.

I opened the door cautiously, just a little, and peered out. You can't be too careful.

A stranger, a fat man who looked foreign.

London swarms with visitors in the summer, people like him. They walk up and down the King's Road, in and out of the shops, crowding the pavements, staring, stopping to take photographs. They wander into our square, often. Sometimes they ring the doorbell.

The street lamp lit his heavy spreading shape, neatly buttoned into a big pastel-coloured suit. Big handkerchief in breast pocket. Small bow tie under rounded fat sallow face. A straw hat held in pudgy hands. Slit eyes.

'Excuse me, lady. Is Mr Lewis at home?'

He stood on our doorstep and wrinkled his fat cheeks into a toothy grin. A friendly stranger, perhaps one of Mischa's fans. I was used to them.

'No,' I said. 'He doesn't live here.'

The visitor tried again.

'Mr Lewis. Gentleman play violin. Mr Mischa Lewis. Have Japanese business correspondence.'

'No. Not here. He lives next door, in the studio. That's his bell, there. He's away. He's playing in Bournemouth and he won't be back till Wednesday night.'

'I am velly solly, lady. Excuse me please. Mr Lewis have letter from Japan?'

'I don't know. He's away. Bournemouth. Not here in London.'

'I am solly. Excuse me please. Good-bye.'

I closed the door.

'What's he want?' called John. He was in the living-room and had just turned off the television. He'd been there all the time and could have saved me the trouble.

'He was Japanese or something and he wanted Mischa. And you are damn lazy.'

'All right, all right,' said John. 'Don't be vile. It was the last of the series and I didn't want to miss the end. Anyway, he wasn't Japanese. He was Chinese.'

'You didn't see him,' I pointed out, 'so you couldn't possibly tell. You were glued to the box. I had to stop working and come down three flights of stairs.'

'But I heard him. Chinese can't say their Rs.' John was knowledgeable for fourteen, and sometimes very boring. 'They say they're velly solly, like him. Japanese can't say Ls. Three frights of stairs, that's what they say.'

'You're velly funny, aren't you.'

I went off to the kitchen and poured myself a drink of the latest in fruit squash. It was said to have pomegranate juice in it, as well as Vitamin C. I added soda and ice and a slice of lemon. Then I forgave John and poured him some too. We took our drinks to the window-seat, a favourite place where we could look out into the square without being seen.

'He's still nosing around, Charcoal,' said John after a while.

Most people call me Char. But John is inventive. He calls me Charlady, Carbon, Carboniferous Substance, Coal and Coke, all sorts of things. I can't stop him.

The fat man was walking ponderously to the corner, looking up at the side wall of our house and the studio nestling below.

Our house was number 23 Nelson Square, Chelsea. The studio where Mischa Lewis lived, was 23A. Someone had built it on years ago, before the parents bought the whole place. We had an ordinary porch with pillars, and a panelled door painted black. The studio had a weird Gothic door studded with iron knobs, and a long passage with stained glass windows, Victorian-style. At the end was a sound-proof room where Mischa practised and slept and ate. It was big and airy. Beyond that was a kitchen and a small bathroom.

Mischa wasn't there a lot that summer. He had come to a vital point in his career as a concert violinist and he was busy playing all over Engand, and broadcasting and getting known. The musical world knew already that he was unusually good. And now the news was spreading. At first a promising unknown, just a name. Then a name with a face you remembered, a personality, someone with talent and energy who might one day be famous. And the gossip columns had mentioned him too. A model girl called Sandy Lovelace had been following him around and their names appeared together in the *Chronicle* and the *Express*. 'Lovely Sandy Lovelace and violinist Mischa Lewis.' People used to turn to look at them in the King's Road, dark romantic Mischa striding along with blonde Sandy. She was tall, taller then he was, a smiling long-legged beauty with a mane of yellow-gold hair. I tried to like her because Mischa did. But I didn't really. I envied her legs and the hair. I am short and square and my dark stringy locks were a great problem just then.

Anyway, Mischa's place was empty that night. And the Chinese stranger stalked up and down under the street lamp, looking at it.

'He's like a big cat,' I said. 'He's got a fat round face and a bow round his neck. He's waiting for the mouse.'

'Chairman Miaow,' said John, and started hooting at his own joke.

'Watch it, he'll hear you.'

But Miaow turned away and padded off into the night. Twenty-three is in the bottom corner of the square and next to it there's a narrow lane, called Lot's Passage, which leads between the sides of other houses down to the Thames. He was going that way.

We opened the window wider and leaned out to see the last of him. There was a big black shiny car parked on the Embankment. Someone sat at the wheel, waiting. The river glistened beyond.

'Bentley,' said John.

Miaow heaved and squeezed his bulk into the passenger seat. He closed the door. The car moved off and out of sight.

I shut the window.

'Come on,' I said. 'Bed-time. The parents will be furious if you're still around when they get back.'

The parents – they are famous for their voyages to distant parts of the world and the travel books they write about them afterwards – were at a dinner at the Marine Society. Their next trip was to be to a small coral island off the coast of Australia. Part of the Great Barrier Reef.

'Pussy cat, pussy cat, where have you been?' chortled John in a falsetto voice as we went upstairs. 'Miaow, miaow!'

'Shut up, you'll wake Tim.'

Tim is our little half-brother.

Our family is complicated.

2

To begin at the beginning, my mother is the well-known journalist Carlotta Firth, of the *Chronicle*, and she met John's father Alan Beresford in the Himalayas. He is a biologist. It was some sort of scientific expedition and she went out to report it for the paper. Nobody would have expected them to have anything in common. But apparently it was instant love.

I'd had two fathers already. The first, my own real father, was a photographer and he died in a motor accident. I can't even remember him. After that my mother married a French film director. She had to divorce him to marry Alan, who was a widower. Alan's first wife, John's mother, had died when John was very small. John had been brought up by housekeepers and nannies until my mother appeared on the scene. There weren't enough aunts and cousins and in-laws on the Beresford side of the family. There were some French relations, the Latour-Beresfords, but they were too far away to help. They lived in France. They were not very interested in Alan and his little boy. Poor John, he didn't have much of a childhood.

Since the Firth-Beresford merger we'd lived happily ever after. After a few fierce battles, that is. John was horrible when I first met him, a scrawny eight-year-old from a stuffy prep school. Grey shorts, grey blazer, grey socks, grey tie and shirt. And grey face. He disgusted me. I was a sophisticated eleven-year-old, used to grown-up company. I had lived a lot of my life in hotels and had flown the Atlantic seven times. I could order meals and shake hands with celebrities. I'd hardly been to school. My mother and I had travelled too much. I could read and write, but that was about all. My education had been of a wider sort. I despised John and his friends and his dreadful prep school jokes.

But I got used to him. And he got used to me. We moved into the big Victorian house in Nelson Square when the parents married. It was the first proper home I'd ever had, with a proper family of my own. By the end of the year the parents had produced Tim, and their first best-seller, *High Mountains*. And they'd found the Bowens, and settled them into the basement flat. Mrs Bowen came in daily and ran our lives. She'd been a nurse in her time. Now she cooked, cleaned, shopped, and looked after baby Tim and John and me. We called her Boney, but she was a comfortable heavyweight. 'Boney only in name,' she would say. She had a husbasd as thin as she was fat. He was a builder and decorator and he would come up and help in his spare time, polishing floors, painting, fixing things. 'Leave it to the old man,' was Boney's answer to that sort of problem.

The parents were always travelling. They would come back with bags full of facts and photographs and tapes, and they would write another book. They went to Colorado and the Sahara and the Gobi, and they wrote *Deserts of Vast Eternity*. They went to South America and India and Africa, Greenland, Canada, Antarctica, round the Horn, up the Amazon. They wrote *Jungle Green*, *Old Man River*, *Eternal Snows*. They were famous and gave lectures and sat on committees and were asked to dinner. And they appeared on television.

That's how they first met Mischa. He'd just won the Paganini Prize and the parents were on the same programme with him in the *Fame Today* series. He was only nineteen, completely unknown. He was the foster child of an elderly couple called Lewis who lived in Norwich, kind simple people who had brought him up strictly. Nobody knew who his real parents were. He'd come from a children's home in Hull. He used to say that he thought his father must have been a Russian sailor. He certainly had an exotic perhaps Russian look, with his dark eyes and high cheek-bones. And then there was his extraordinary musical gift. Where did that come from? He seemed to have an inborn knowledge of the violin. Mr Lewis, his foster father, ran a music shop and was a violinist himself in a scratchy sort of way. So there were always instruments available and people who loved music. Little Mischa learned very young, and when he was ten he and his foster father used to play in a string quartet with some friends, Mr Lewis as first violin and Mischa as second. Soon it became obvious that Mischa was easily the better violinist, so they changed places. The violin became the most important thing in his life. He got a grant when he was twelve and studied seriously, at a violin school.

When the parents first met him, he was an orphan once more. Mr and Mrs Lewis were both dead and Mischa was alone in the world. In spite of the ups and down of his life he was a steady person, and humorous and kind. The parents liked him. The studio was empty. My mother bullied Alan until he halved the rent, and Mischa moved in. The place became his home, his personal refuge where he lived and worked and relaxed, and to which he returned gratefully after travels abroad. He went away to Paris for a year and studied there, and then to San Francisco. He was twenty-four now. He'd played at a Prom, that summer, and in February he would be making his first appearance in the Festival Hall. After that, there might be all sorts of chances, recording and concerts abroad. We were very proud of him and regarded him as part of our family.

Actually Mischa and I had some things in common. I'd never known a real father. And I too had a hidden talent. Nothing creative, not like Mischa's music. Just my maths. It was Alan, my step-father, who first took my education seriously. I'd always loathed schools. I was never at one for long, and I ran away from quite a few of them. Then Alan came into my life and said I might have a brain. 'You don't have your mother's staggering good looks,' he said bluntly. 'But perhaps there's something lurking inside that odd-shaped head of yours.' He chose a London day-school for me, and coached me until I was way out in front of the class. I loved it. I felt I had grown wings. By the time I was sixteen they were saying I was a mathematical genius and would probably get a place at Cambridge. Alan began to wonder if he'd pushed me too hard, and urged me to let up. 'Don't work too hard, Charlotte.' But I couldn't stop.

John was a different sort of person, intelligent but easygoing to the point of laziness. He was now in his second year at Alan's old school. 'This well-endowed boy could do much better,' one of his reports said. He didn't care. He did just enough work to get by and no more. He would probably get into some university or other by the same narrow margin. No one had to tell John not to work too hard.

3

On Thursday morning I remembered that Mischa would be back from Bournemouth. We were not allowed to disturb him when he was practising, so I had to wait till eleven when I knew he took a break. I called him on the house telephone and explained about Chairman Miaow.

'Chinese?' he queried.

'Yes. Well, John says Chinese.'

'Couldn't be. I'm expecting a Japanese, I think. I've had a letter about him. I'll bring it through. Any coffee in your kitchen?'

The studio and number 23 were separate households, but there was one small corner where they connected, and that was through the broom cupboard in the kitchen. Boney's husband, the old man, had made this door so that Boney could go straight through to clean the studio without going outside into the square. And she had been cursing him ever since because it was a low narrow door and she found it a tight squeeze for her size. We used to be able to hear Mischa playing from inside the cupboard. The old man hadn't made his door quite sound-proof. Tim liked to sit in there, with a teddy for company, listening to the endless ribbon of violin music. He became an expert. While he was growing up Mischa was busy expanding his repertoire, studying the great violin concertos and sonatas. Music poured over Tim's little head. Beethoven, Bach, Fauré, César Franck, Mozart, Sibelius, Bruch, Mendelssohn. 'What's that?' Tim would say. 'I like it.' And Mischa would tell him. Most children sing, little tunes of their own or nursery rhymes or pop songs, but Tim was different. He sang classics, bits of violin sonatas, romances, concertos, studies.

I put on the coffee and Mischa came through the cupboard, past the brushes and dustpans, dodging the Hoover, holding his arms tight to his sides so as not to knock down any of Boney's tins of polish. He was medium tall, rather thin, with a natural unaffected manner which made him quite ordinary to meet. You would never have known he was a genius. He saved his energy and seriousness for the most important thing in his life, playing the violin. With us he would be completely relaxed, just our old friend Mischa, a sort of big brother. The dark eyes under straight black brows would shine with humour, and he would be silly and friendly and full of jokes. But when he picked up his instrument and bent his head over it to play, he became a different person. The smiling eyes would narrow until they became pinpoints of light, or they would dilate and glare with what seemed like anger. His eyebrows would meet in a frown of concentration, or lift above lowered eyelids as if he were listening, and dreaming, while the music flowed on without him. He was far away from us then, another Mischa, wrapped in the secret mysteries of his art. He seemed to have forgotten all about us and the unimportant things of everyday life.

We sat at the kitchen table that morning, with mugs of coffee and a packet of biscuits. Tim was already there, puzzling over a comic and dropping biscuit crumbs. He was just seven and could read, muttering aloud as he went, an annoying habit which he said was absolutely essential. Without it he couldn't read at all. John, who believed that going to boarding-school entitled you to extra rest in the holidays, was still in bed. Boney had gone out shopping. Alan my stepfather was in the British Museum. My mother was at work in the *Chronicle's* offices in Fleet Street.

'This all began,' said Mischa, holding out the flimsy airmail envelope with a Japanese stamp on it, 'a long time ago. It began with Mrs Rose Kawate.'

'Who's she?'

'She was a friend in San Francisco.' Mischa made a Japanese face and rolled his eyes. 'Very kind Japanese lady.'

'They can't say their Ls,' I remembered.

'You're right. A very kind Japanese ray-dee,rivving in San Francisco. Invites poor student Mischa Rewis to her ruvvery house.' He rolled his eyes some more, got up and bowed, and showed an imaginary poor student through an imaginary door.

Tim noticed there was something interesting going on and abandoned his comic.

'Do that again, Mischa. Make that face with your eyes.'

'Poor student,' went on Mischa, taking up an imaginary violin. 'He go to ruvvery house of Mrs Kawate and pray vio-rin. He pray many wrong sonatas and Mrs Kawate pray piano.' He sat down again and played the piano on the kitchen table and Tim joined in and had to be restrained so that Mischa could go on with the story. 'She pray piano very beautyfurry. Ruvvery accompanist. She say one day she go back to Japan, she send Mr Rewis first crass vio-rin. Itarry-an vio-rin. Varruable antique.'

'Pity she never did.' I knew that Mischa wanted an Italian violin more than anything in the world. A Stradivarius, a Guarnerius, a Landolfi. But he was poor and it would be some time before he could afford one.

'Ah, but wait a minute,' said Mischa. 'Poor student Mr Rewis go back to Ing-rand. Sometimes write retters to Japan-ese ray-dee. She reeve San Francisco, she go back Japan. She sick, she have disease in her rungs. One day so very sick. Doctor come. It is too rate!'

'Too rate!' echoed Tim, spell-bound.

'She ray down and die!' finished Mischa. He rolled his eyes violently, coughed and spluttered, fell from his chair and lay corpse-like on the floor. Tim fell on top of him and it was some time before order was restored and we sat down at the table again.

Then Mischa gave me the letter from Japan. It was type-written on a small piece of white silky paper. I read it to myself in Japanese style, changing the Ls to Rs. Aloud it would have sounded like this —

> Mitsura Export-Import
> Tokyo
> Japan

Dear Sirs,

We have pressure to inform you that regal representative of Mrs Rose Kawate have handed us antique instrument for des-patch to you. Deceased ray-dee say goods is of Itarryan maker Guarnerius. For convenience of handring we forward item to you in good condition packed with six other instruments of Japan manufacture. Our British office immediate-ry will correct six be-ronging to him, his name Mr Yamaguchi. Date of shipping to be announced rater.

> Yours faithfurry —

There was no signature.

'What's it say?' asked Tim, hoping for some more fun.

'I'm getting a present from Japan,' said Mischa, finishing his coffee and getting up to go.

I gave him back the letter.

'But it's wonderful, isn't it Mischa? It's just what you've always wanted.'

He shook his head regretfully. 'It couldn't be a real one, Char. The world's full of fake violins, Strads and Guarnerii. They used to make them in Germany, just like the real thing. Labels and all.'

'Rabels,' I corrected.

'Rabels,' he agreed. 'Now they're making them in Japan, even better. Mrs Kawate was a good pianist, but I don't think she knew anything about violins. Too bad. You can have it, Tim. It's certain to be a fake, but it would do for you to begin on.'

Tim's face lit up.

'True? Not joking?'

'True. You'll have to grow a bit. And get some more muscle here,' added Mischa, pinching Tim's scrawny arm. 'You need it for bowing. And you need a strong chin to hold the violin. There.'

'I could play it on the floor, like a cello.'

'Not if I'm around, you won't. Thanks for the coffee, Char. See you.'

'Stay for lunch, Mischa,' said Tim, hanging on to his leg. 'Runch, I mean. Stay for runch.'

'I can't,' said Mischa. 'I'm having runch with ruvvery Sandy Ruv-race.'

4

September came. Misty mornings, golden sunny days, cold nights. John packed his trunk and went back to school. The parents were very busy, meeting people, planning, making endless lists of things they'd need on the Great Barrier Reef.

I took Tim to school on the first day of term.

'And where are you off to, my friend?' asked Fred the milkman, dropping five bottles off his fingers into the plastic crates in his truck.

'School!' shouted Tim. 'New school!'

'And what's that you wearing today?' asked Geraldine, our West Indian traffic warden.

'My blazer!' Tim stuck out his thin chest. 'My new blazer, and my cap and tie!'

'My, you smart kid!' said Geraldine, strolling past on long brown legs.

'Good morning to you! Lovely day!' boomed our neighbour the Admiral. 'Back to school?'

He isn't really an Admiral. During the war he was a First Lieutenant RNVR. Now he's an author and writes books about boats and has a naval manner. He always shouts when he meets you outdoors, as if he were on the bridge of his destroyer in a Force 8 gale. He is a widower and lives alone with his dog Skipper, a big black labrador.

'Yes,' we said, patting Skipper. 'Back to school.'

'That's a splendid rig, Tim,' said the Admiral. 'Jolly good show!'

We marched proudly the length of the square.

'Morning all,' said Mick, who keeps a fruit and vegetable barrow on the corner of the King's Road. 'Going back to school, then?'

'Tim is,' I explained. 'I'm only going two days a week this term, because I'm working for university. The other days I have coaching and I work at home.'

'Cor. Well, all I can say is good luck. You write exams for it then?'

'Yes. In November. Then they interview you if you're good enough.'

'Cor. Never could do that sort of thing. Exams and that.'

5

Mischa went to Cheltenham and Newcastle and Glasgow. The tourists drifted away, back to their own cities all over the world. The King's Road settled down for the winter.

The doorbell, one sunny morning.

'Excuse preeze. Mr Rewis at home?'

Three of them. Flashy teeth with gold stoppings. Eyelids drooping over small dark eyes. Dark hats and overcoats.

'No. He lives next-door, in the studio. That's his bell. You're not Mr – er – Nagasaki, by any chance?'

'Yamaguchi.' He bowed. The other two grinned. 'Is not in house, Mr Rewis?'

'No. Not in London. Glasgow.'

'Pray vio-rin in Grass-grow? Back soon?'

'Back Saturday.'

They got into a small black car, a foreign one, and drove away. I left a note for Mischa. Next time I saw him he said Mr Yamaguchi had telephoned. The violins were coming in December. Mr Yamaguchi was going to open a music boutique in the King's Road in the New Year, and there would be more things coming later.

'What sort of things?'

'Records, sheet music, instruments. The Japanese make very good violins, actually,' said Mischa. 'And they're wonderful musicians. They play our music, and we can't even understand theirs. Same with Chinese.'

'But why is he dumping the violins in your studio? Only one of them is for you.'

'It doesn't bother me, Char. Actually they're saving me trouble. I'll get my fake Guarnerius through Customs and delivered to the door. And they're paying the freight.'

'He could have had them delivered to his shop.'

'He hasn't got a shop yet. He's looking for one.'

I saw Mr Yamaguchi several times in the King's Road. Sometimes his car was parked in Nelson Square. His friends would be sitting inside, reading newspapers.

Geraldine came round the corner just too late. She'd missed them again.

'My, that Honda!' she said. 'When he sees me coming, he drives away. You wait, next time I get him and write a ticket.'

'Write me one too,' said Fred the milkman. 'Geraldine loves Fred. Go on. I'll stick it on my truck.'

'Cheeky, you are,' said Geraldine.

The Admiral noticed the Honda too.

'Funny chaps, Japs,' he said. 'Damn clever, too. Cars, motorbikes, you name it, they make it. They'll capture the market if we don't look out. Work going all right?'

'Yes, not bad.'

'Best of luck.'

'Thanks.'

'Good show,' he said. 'To heel, Skipper!'

'Chinks, are they?' said Mick the barrow-boy. 'What they want then? I seed them coming to your door.'

'They're Japanese, Mick. They came about some violins. They're going to start a boutique.'

'Cor. Can't stand them violins. No offence. I'll have to bring me ear plugs.'

6

October.

Bright skies, a cold wind blowing leaves before it.

Boney's old man turned on the central heating. The house was snug and warm, littered with radio sets, collapsible boats, tents, packaged foods, medicines, collecting-boxes, fish-hooks, ropes, diving equipment. The parents buzzed happily among these things. Boney tried to clean round them and grumbled, mildly. Tim wanted to open everything and see how it worked and was warned off more than once. Finally he decided no one would mind if he took a box of old-fashioned glass slides to the window-seat and held them up to the light.

'Hands off, you little monkey!' shouted Alan, so suddenly that Tim dropped the slide he was holding. It cracked as it hit the floor. 'My God, can't someone find something else for this child to do? We'll never be ready at this rate. It's October. We should be in a state of advanced preparedness. All this stuff must be shipped by the end of the week. Lucky that slide wasn't an important one.'

Tim whimpered apologies and shuffled off, wiping his eyes on his cuff. He was going to his refuge in time of trouble, the broom cupboard. Mischa was in the studio practising Brahms sonatas with his friend John Mackintosh, known as Mac. They had done some Beethoven sonatas together for radio. They were working up the Brahms for another recital.

'Brahms is a bit sad for me,' said Tim when he reappeared later. 'I like Bait-over better. Especially with Mac on the piano.'

'Beethoven, you mean.'

'Yes. I like the Bait-over Concerto, the last movement. It goes like this.' He sang, correctly, the opening phrase of the *rondo*. 'It's like a little trumpet starting up.'

'Silly old Tim. It's a violin, not a trumpet.'

'I know that. But it's a trumpet sort of tune.'

A few days later I quarrelled with Graham, my boyfriend. It was about nothing. He came to say goodbye. I got annoyed with him, hanging about looking awkward. I said I might be too busy to write. He said not to bother then. He went away, to Leeds University.

I threw a scarf round my neck and leaned against the wind as I made my way down the square.

'Good afternoon!' roared the Admiral. 'Stiffish breeze!'

I nodded and turned briskly into the King's Road. My eyes were stinging. A lump of misery sat on my chest. What a fool I'd been, saying those stupid things. Poor old Graham. He must have thought I was out of my mind. Not that it mattered what he thought. I would never see him again.

The only boyfriend I'd ever had.

As I passed the Pizza Palace I saw Mischa, sitting alone at a table. He banged on the window-pane and beckoned me to come in and join him.

'Come on, Char. Have some coffee.'

'All right then. Black.'

'What's the matter? Worried about your exam?'

I told him about Graham.

'Well, that's two of us then,' he said cheerfully. 'Lovely Sandy Lovelace has just walked out on me. She's interested in a TV producer now. She couldn't wait for me to get famous. Said it might never happen.'

'Mischa! That's horrible!'

I was too proud to write to Graham and say I was sorry. I worked and worked. I got tired and cross and stale. Alan took me for a walk along the Embankment one evening after dinner and spoke seriously.

'Don't work at night. Watch television. Go to a film or something. Play records. Ring up your friends. Anything you like, but no books after six o'clock.'

The night sky was heavy with cloud. The river swirled dark and oily below us, far below. The tide was out. Black muddy banks were showing, and pieces of mud-coated rubbish, old bicycle wheels, prams, bits of wood.

'I'm sorry, Alan. I was horrible at dinner. I'm sorry.'

'You're overworking, that's all. Now look at Mischa. That's how you should do it. He works regular hours, by the clock, and no nonsense. You never hear him playing at night, do you? Except on the concert platform. You must discipline yourself.'

I said I'd try it.

We turned home. Just before we reached Lot's Passage I saw a very big fat man, a man I'd seen before, walking slowly away from us, past the street lamp, on into the darkness beyond it. Chairman Miaow. It was a cold night and he was wearing a heavy overcoat with a belt round his bulging middle. There was a girl with him, tall and golden-haired.

27

For a moment I thought it was Sandy Lovelace. But I could have been wrong.

Anyway, what could they possibly have in common?

7

'Happy birthday, Charlotte.'

The parents smiled and kissed me.

'Open them, open them!' cried Tim, jumping up and down.

The pile of presents on the breakfast table was all mine. It was Saturday, so no one was in a hurry. I opened them slowly and with great pleasure. Two envelopes with money from godparents. Some cards from schoolfriends. A hand-knitted sweater from Boney. A pair of wooden book-ends from John, made last term at school. A Victorian brass candlestick, with snuffer, from Mischa. The LP I'd been saving up for from Alan. A box of chocolate mints from Tim, because he was so fond of them himself. Nothing from Graham.

I opened my mother's present last because it was the biggest. Good, she'd got me one of the fur hats which everybody was wearing that year, and which she knew I wanted. Underneath was something bulky. I lifted more fluffy tissue paper and looked. A tweed coat, fashionable, elegant, not at all the sort of thing I usually wore.

'Mummy, lovely. Thank you,' I said automatically, fingering a sleeve. 'But it's so smart. I mean, I've still got my old one. And my anorak.'

'Darling, I know. But you're going to need it. For France.'

'France?' What could she be talking about? I wasn't going to France.

'For Christmas, darling. It's a surprise, I know. The French side of Alan's family, you remember, the Latour-Beresfords? They've very kindly offered –'

'You mean we're not having Christmas here?'

'Well, not this year, darling. You see –'

'And me?' put in Tim, who had a horror of being left out. 'What about me?'

'Yes, you too Tim. And John. They've invited you for Christmas in this lovely château. It is lovely, isn't it, Alan.'

Alan emerged briefly from *The Times*. 'Wonderful place. Tout confort. She's a good sort, ma French cousine.'

I looked at them aghast. Anger rose inside.

'You mean you're not going to be there? What sort of Christmas do you think we'll have without you, with people we've never even met? Where the hell are you going to be?'

Alan abandoned the newspaper and glared at me. I pulled the coat from its box, scattering tissue, and shook it furiously in their faces.

'I tell you I'm not going to France for Christmas without you! I don't care if you give me twenty blasted coats, I'm not going! I want Christmas at home, like we always have –'

'Charlotte! Pull yourself together! For heaven's sake, let's be rational about it –'

'Darling, don't you see. We'll be on the Great Barrier Reef –'

'Oh *no!* That's the end!'

I flung the coat on the floor. Tim burst into tears and my mother had to take him on her knee. The presents lay in disorder, wrappings everywhere. Coffee got cold. Tempers got hot. I knew I was being impossible, but I couldn't stop.

Christmas away from home, no parents, complete strangers, everything upset. And telling me on my birthday too.

Alan took charge and gradually got us sane again. The things they wanted particularly to see, he explained, would be at their best over Christmas. It would be winter with us, but down under everything would be flourishing. A certain fish would be breeding, and some sea-bird would be making its annual visit to that part of the Reef. Crabs would be migrating. Currents would be ideal for studying these activities, and so would tides. Equipment could be landed.

All this in his calmest and most professional voice. And they'd thought of various relations who might have us for Christmas – I groaned rudely at that – and had decided that the Latour-Beresfords would be the most fun. We'd fly to Paris and be driven on southwards to the château. Tim cheered up. He'd never flown before.

Alan always manages to get round me. He's a good stepfather. I apologized, eventually, and they apologized. I put on the new coat and they exclaimed that I looked lovely, older, taller. Well, perhaps it wouldn't be so dreadful having a different sort of Christmas.

Later I paraded in the kitchen for Boney, wearing the sweater she'd knitted for me. She put her hands on her enormous hips and surveyed me critically.

'You look really nice in it, Charlotte, though I say it myself.'

'Boney, it's lovely. It's the best thing this birthday.'

I told her about Christmas, and the row.

'I know dear. I heard you going on. I couldn't help it. Never mind. It'll be lovely there, won't it.'

'I suppose so. Where are you going, Boney?'

'Me and the old man are going to Derby, to his sister's. It's ever so nice there, we haven't been for years. We've promised. Look, here's your birthday horoscope.'

She spread out the *Daily Express* for me to read.

'A year of success for those interested in sport and finance. You are certainly a dark horse and will surprise those around you. Old friendships will bring happiness in the New Year.'

'Thank you, Boney. They don't tell you much, do they?'

Graham would be back in London for Christmas, and I would be in France. But he probably wouldn't come and see me anyway, so perhaps it was just as well. I couldn't care less.

'Dear John,' I wrote. 'The book-ends are the greatest thing since the invention of the wheel. I really like them. They are propping up calculus at this moment. They've probably written to you about Christmas. I was furious, but I suppose we have to go. The *Chronicle* came on Tuesday and took photographs for the new series. They said just be natural, do what we usually do. So Tim showed off terribly and tried to get in all the pictures. The Japanese who wrote to Mischa are going to start a music boutique in the King's Road. They hang about the square in a Honda. Also seen your old friend Miaow down Lot's Passage, without the Rolls. Mischa has broken off with the lovely Sandy Lovelace. Love Char.'

'Dear Charcoal Biscuit, I am grad to get your retter because I am in bed with frew. They say I can get up rater today. Actually I am rooking forward to frying to France. I went to that château years ago with Aran. We were on a camping trip. The Honda is a first class machine actually. A chap in the house has a Honda bike at home. You can tell Japanese by their eyelids, they hang over their eyes. Chinese eyes slant. It wasn't a Rolls, it was a Bentley. Yr step bro Jo.'

Cold days. Wet days. Fog. Black trees standing leafless against grey skies. Tim, after a lot of fuss, was persuaded to put his blazer aside for the spring and wear something heavier.

I disciplined myself. I worked to a time-table, like Mischa. He had a fur hat, like the one my mother had given me for my birthday. We would put on our hats, pull them down to our eyebrows, and go out walking for forty-five minutes every day. We wiped drips from our noses and hunched our shoulders against the cold. My hair straggled over the collar of my friendly old overcoat.

Over the bridge to Battersea Park we trudged, and back again, along the Embankment, where the houseboats swayed gently together in icy mist. They were sad and uncared-for. Paint was peeling. Dead frostbitten plants drooped from window-boxes. Dirty curtains hung inside tarnished port-holes. There was a damp Thames smell.

'Sandy used to live there,' said Mischa, pointing. 'That blue one, right out there beyond the barge. She rented it from a friend.'

'Who has it now?'

'I don't know. It's all covered up, isn't it. It was mostly for parties, in the summer.'

The little blue houseboat had tarpaulin spread over its decks and roped down all round. The mermaid on the prow poked her head out, as if trying to swim free.

'Where does Sandy live now?'

'I don't know, Char. She's got a flat somewhere. It's all over. I don't want to see her. I don't want to have anything more to do with her. Or her friends.'

'I'm sorry, Mischa.'

'I didn't realize at first,' he said. 'She's part of a really bad set.'

'You mean orgies?' I asked hopefully. 'Go on. Tell me. I'm not a baby.'

'Not orgies really. Drugs.'

'Hard stuff?'

'Yes. Hard stuff.'

8

November.

John came home for half-term. He and Tim spent pocket-money on fireworks which we took to Hampstead and let off with some friends. There was a bonfire and sausages on sticks. John was in a state of wild excitement the whole weekend, ate prodigiously, went to two films, watched too much television, telephoned his friends. When he wasn't doing anything else he talked non-stop about school. He bored us all dreadfully.

'Darling, about Christmas,' said my mother, ruffling his hair.

'What, what?' said John. 'Sorry, I was listening to telly.'

'Christmas. You know we're leaving on the sixteenth, don't you? So you'll be back before we go, just. And you're booked to fly to Paris on the twentieth, you and Char and Tim –'

'That's fine,' said John, his eyes still glued to the screen.

'And I'm doing all your packing for you except a few last-minute essentials, and Boney will have a list of them. You remember your great-aunt Clothilde, dear, don't you? And great-uncle Maurice? Then there's Madeleine, their one and only. And there'll be all the cousins, more your age. Boys and girls. You remember Madeleine, John?'

'Yes, of course.'

'Madeleine is at Edinburgh University and she's going on the same flight as you. And when you get to Orly there will be a car, and she'll drive you all the way to the château. It will be fun, darling, won't it? There's a boar hunt on Christmas Day, every year –'

'Marvellous,' said John.

I took him to Waterloo to catch his train back to school. The platform was full of boys heading for the same place, most of them much older than John. He suddenly looked small and gloomy.

'About Christmas,' he said. 'They're awfully grand, those French relations. I don't know what sort of time we'll have.'

'We'll have fun,' I told him.

'My French is très mauvais,' he explained. 'I'll look a fool.'

'No you won't. Don't speak too much, that's all. Just hunt boars.'

'Bores, ha-ha. Actually Great-aunt Clothilde is a terrifying bore. Wait till you see her. Silly name, Clothilde.' He giggled and cheered up. 'Great-aunt Clot.'

'What's Madeleine like? I asked. 'The girl.'

'Beastly. Got red hair. And she's not a girl any more. She must be about thirty now. Or older.'

'She couldn't be all that old. She's a student at Edinburgh University.' I had listened to my mother's briefing more carefully than he had.

He caught sight of a friend and obviously didn't want me there any more.

'There's Sparkers,' he said. 'Don't wait. Au revoir.'

'Au revoir. Write if you have a moment.'

'Oui, oui. Same to you. I say, when's your exam?'

'Three weeks. But I won't know the results till Christmas.'

'Good luck, Carbon.'

'Thanks. Bye.'

'Bye.'

'I tell you one thing,' said Mick, shovelling brussels sprouts into my shopping-bag. 'Just one thing. Nobody's going to start no music boutique in the King's Road unless the big boss says so.'

Fred had parked his truck alongside Mick's barrow, blocking the entrance to the square. Geraldine, in thick winter overcoat and black shiny boots, a woolly scarf under her peaked cap, strolled over and joined in.

'Who's this big boss then?' she asked.

'It's Mr Lee, sweetheart,' said Fred. 'You know him. Big and beefy. Owns the Chinese resterong and the Karate Klub and the Judo.Jim. Owns half the shops in the King's Road.'

'I know that man,' said Geraldine. 'My, he must be a rich man.'

'Rich, cor,' said Mick. 'He's so rich he don't know what to do with it. Did you say pound of carrots, luv?'

'If I were Mr Lee,' said Fred, squeezing Geraldine's waist, 'I'd take you to the pictures, not half I wouldn't. In my big Bentley.'

Two cars were lined up behind Fred's truck, unable to get any further. The driver of the front one rolled down his window. The car behind was hooting angrily.

'I say, milkman, do you mind? Some of us are trying to get past, don't you know.'

'All right sir. All right. Keep your hair on. I've got my work to do same as other people, haven't I.' Fred gave us a huge wink, got back into his truck and drove it very slowly down the middle of the street, the cars revving impatiently behind him.

'He's cheeky, that Fred,' said Geraldine, taking out her notebook and moving on. 'Definitely.'

'That'll be forty-two new pence, with the onions,' said Mick. 'Thank you luv.'

'What's he look like, Mick?' I asked. 'That Mr Lee.'

'He's a Chink. Come from Hong Kong. Seen him up and down the King's Road, often.'

'Big and fat?'

'That's him. Got slitty eyes, like this.' Mick stretched his eyelids with calloused fingers. 'And I tell you something else, as your old friend. Just keep out of his way, that's all.'

'Why?'

'He don't like anyone interfering, our Mr Lee. Not in the King's Road he don't. Those Nips will have to watch it. I'm telling you. Cor.'

'I'm getting a violin,' Tim told the Admiral. 'Or I might. If it's a real one I'm going to give it to Mischa, but if it's not a real one I'm going to keep it.'

'Lucky Tim,' said the Admiral. 'Good show.'

Three days till my exam. I was jumpy and bad-tempered, not hungry, sleeping badly.

Boney had cooked me something special which she thought would tempt me. 'Go on, try it,' she said. 'It'll do you good.'

'Don't look at a single book over the weekend,' said Alan.

'She's tired,' said my mother.

'It's that Graham, if you ask me,' Boney murmured.

They were all kind. They petted and fussed. When they thought I wasn't listening they discussed my chances. They wondered what the other candidates were like this year, and which schools they'd been to, and whether exams weren't a mistake anyway.

I told Alan I felt like a race-horse.

'You are one,' he said. 'I'm putting you in for the Derby and I hope you win.'

The papers were dreadful. I couldn't believe my eyes. Much more difficult than any of those I'd practised on. My pen leaked. The desk they gave me was rickety. Afterwards, gloomy post-mortems with my teacher and people from the school. No one had ever seen such questions, not in all their experience. None of us would get in, even if we got interviews.

We went to Brighton for the weekend and stayed with friends, the parents and Mischa and me. Mischa played at the Dome. It was the Mendelssohn concerto.

'Sentimental,' said my mother, who liked Bach and Mozart best.

Mendelssohn was perfect for my mood. Delicious sweetness spun from Mischa's violin, threads of silky caramel sugar. I was so tired, so glad to stop working. I felt like crying.

Next day we walked on the cliffs in wintry sunshine. The sea was pale silver, whipped into foam at the crest of each wave. A strong salty wind roared in our ears and blew our conversation away. We could hardly hear each other.

'Don't worry, darling!' shouted my mother. 'If you don't get in there are lots of other things in life!'

'Yes!' yelled Mischa. 'But not the things she wants — if you want something badly enough you have to go on trying!'

'You're right!' I yelled back. 'I'll have to go on trying!'

9

The first day of December.

The heavy equipment for the Firth-Beresford expedition to the Great Barrier Reef, which had left Nelson Square in October, had arrived safely in Cleveland Bay, Queensland, Australia, much to Alan's relief. It was waiting, crated, labelled, listed, on board the ocean-going tug *Australian Princess* which was to be the base ship. The rest of the parents' luggage accumulated in the hall. Rucksacks with clothes to wear when they were there, suitcases with better clothes to wear when they came back, cameras, typewriters, notebooks, and a new sort of glass-bottomed boat packed in two huge boxes which had arrived too late to go with the other stuff. My mother's secretary, Miss Margaret Robson, commonly known as Bobby, was installed in the study and answered the telephone, typed letters and took dictation all day for days on end.

'Where does this go, Bobby?' I held up a package marked FIRTH-BERESFORD-URGENT which the postman had just delivered.

'Lord,' said Bobby. 'One more parcel and I'll go mad.'

We were in the *Chronicle*'s weekend supplement, in the first of a series about the Great Barrier Reef trip. The article was headed *Where Are You Going For Christmas?* Tim cut out the page which included his photograph and hung it above his bed.

The telephone and the doorbell rang constantly. Friends, reporters, photographers, letters, parcels. And carol singers.

'Away in a manger and away with you!' roared Alan furiously, flinging open the front door. He was expecting another important parcel in the post, but it was just two shabby kids cowering terrified in the porch. They'd sung one verse at breakneck speed, starting on different notes. 'Call yourselves carol singers! You're nothing but little nuisances! Go on, go away!'

They shuffled off with backward looks and Alan banged the door.

'Sorry,' he said, simmering down. 'But honestly, you can't let them get away with it. They should practise first, instead of inflicting that disgraceful performance on us. Now, where's my list?'

In the King's Road the shops glittered and sparkled with Christmas things, toys and toiletries and clothes and bottles of wine, decorated with red ribbons and aritficial snowflakes. Pink turkeys hung in the butcher's. Coloured lights burned night and day. Mick had holly and mistletoe on his barrow, and a pile of small Christmas trees leaning up against the wall by his side.

Tim and I went shopping for presents. The pavements were crammed with people, pushing, standing, hurrying, dawdling, all hunting for the perfect gift and the paper to wrap it in. And the red sticky-tape to fasten it, adorned with an endless row of tiny angels. The label, and the plastic bow. And the perfect Christmas card, birds on a branch of apple blossom, or a stage-coach rolling through the snow full of poke-bonneted ladies. Or Wise Men, Madonnas, rows of cherubic choirboys, or views of Westminster Abbey. Our family Christmas card had gone off weeks ago, under Bobby's direction, a photograph of a particularly beautiful piece of white coral against a red background. I liked it. It had a feeling of Christmas. I'd sent it to lots of friends, but not Graham. He hadn't sent me one. I hadn't heard from him at all.

I saw Sandy Lovelace, coming out of the Pop Shop. I wanted to walk past but Tim tugged my hand.

'There's Sandy!' he cried joyfully. 'Sandy!'

'Tim, angel! And Charlotte!' She was wearing a golden fur. Her hair spread over and mingled with it. She was glorious, animal-like. I hated her. 'Darlings, I haven't seen you for so long! How are you?'

'I'm fine,' said Tim. 'I'm at a new school, we have French and P.E. and I am in Form One. And we're going to France for Christmas!'

'Darling, really? Going to France? How simply lovely! When?'

She bent down and put her furry arm round Tim. Green eyes narrowed ever so slightly. Long lashes quivered.

'Come on Tim,' I said. 'We've got to go.' No business of hers when we went to France.

'The twentieth!' said Tim, proud that he'd remembered. 'In a aeroplane. Flying!'

'How exciting, Tim! And you, Char?'

I looked fixedly at the shoes in the nearest window and pretended not to hear.

'Charlotte too and John,' said Tim, unsquashable. 'And Boney and her old man are going to Derby. And Mummy and Alan to Australia!'

'Such fun, Tim!' Hateful false smile, false person altogether. How Mischa had ever liked her I couldn't understand. 'I read all about Mummy and Alan in the *Chronicle*, and I saw a picture of you.'

'You'll be late for telly, Tim,' I said.

'And you know what I'm getting?' Tim watched Sandy closely to see the effect. 'A violin! And it might be a real one and Mischa will keep it. But if it's not a real one he's going to give it to me.'

'A real violin?' Sandy was all attention.

'It might be a – er. What might it be, Charlotte?' He was stuck.

'Oh it's all nonsense really,' I explained. 'Some old crank is sending Mischa a violin. It's not real. It's a fake Guarnerius. Come on, Tim.'

Sandy said good-bye and got into her Mini. Cars were like jewels that year, bronze, green, purple and gold, iridescent and glittering. Hers was gold, naturally, with windows in black no-see glass. She slammed the door and disappeared, a bad fairy in a magic box.

'She's lovely!' cried Tim, skipping ahead into the square. 'Lovely Sandy Lovelace, lovely, lovely!'

He ran the rest of the way. I followed, laden with parcels.

10

They sent for me. I'd got an interview. Two of us went from school, me and a very dull girl who wanted to read geography. We felt very young and lonely. We walked about Cambridge, looking at colleges and getting lost. Everyone had bicycles, except us. It was cold and windy. The geographer said East Anglia was very exposed. The wind came straight from the Ural Mountains.

Dons talked to me and asked me about my papers and my hobbies. I was very nervous and couldn't think of anything interesting to say. They smiled kindly and thanked me for coming.

'Dear Carbohydrate. Clever you, got an interview. Our exams have been vile, viler, vilest this term. But we won the house football. I managed to get a super stamp album second-hand from someone in the house. It will do for Tim's Xmas present. It has quite a few useful stamps in it already. If Tim doesn't like it I can look after it for him until he is older. Rather kind of me, don't you think. J. Beresford.'

'Dear John. Our exams were viler than vile. So although I got an interview I don't think I will get in. I may have to try again next term. The parents want to open some of the presents with us before they go. And the others are for when we come back from France. With any luck your grand relations will give us few expensive cadeaux too, so there will be a continuous rustle of wrapping-paper from now till next year. Mischa played well at Brighton. Tim and I saw Sandy Lovelace in the King's Road. I'm sure he'll like the stamp album. See you next week. C Firth. PS Mick the Barrow says Chairman Miaow is called Lee and owns half the King's Road, at least I'm sure it must be the same person.'

John came home. The hall was already crowded with luggage and parcels and letters and Christmas cards. John opened his trunk to extract 'some surprises,' he said, and added dirty clothes and muddy football boots to the confusion.

There was excitement in the air. Christmas was coming. Our tickets and passports were ready for France, and in each of our rooms upstairs was a neatly-packed suitcase with a list on top of it of things which still had to be put in. John rushed up and down the stairs, turned on the radio, turned on the television, put on records, forgot to turn off the things he wasn't listening to. Tim rushed behind him, squeaking. Alan tried not to lose his temper. My mother seemed to spend all day dictating letters to poor Bobby, who got more and more behind typing them. 'Lord,' she said. 'I'll never be through.' Boney heaved sighs and went on with her work, muttering that when we'd all gone she'd be able to clear up properly and about time too.

On the parents' last evening we had a party. I wore the dress my mother was giving me for Christmas. It was perfect, because I had chosen it myself. After the incident with the birthday coat this seemed the best way. She was kind, and said again that I looked lovely, older, taller. Downstairs in the sitting-room, just the five of us, we opened our special family presents. Tim got the two-wheeler he'd been begging for. It had been hidden in the basement where only Boney and the old man could see it. John got a microscope, an old one of Alan's, and a stop-watch and a black leather waist-coat. Besides the dress, I got a hairy Irish rug for my bed. I really liked it. So did Tim, and he put it over himself and turned into a hairy caterpillar which humped itself along the floor. So I told him if he was going to be a caterpillar I would have his bike, which changed him back into a boy pretty quickly. Then John produced his surprises, the hand-made ones which always get a round of applause. There was a pottery bowl for my mother with her initials on it. And for Alan there was a box for fishing flies. And there was a bigger box for Tim, with a padlock, and inside was the second-hand stamp album which John had written about. And a medium-sized box for me, which John said I could take to university. 'Or anywhere else,' he added tactfully.

Then I gave Tim a plastic Roman helmet, and Alan a print of Captain Cook landing in Australia, and John a record token, and my mother a framed picture which I had made myself out of a Beatrix Potter postcard. I'd cut out the faces of the Flopsy Bunnies and put photographs of John and Tim and me instead. We looked much better with long ears, everyone agreed. And Tim produced his presents, which were bulgy as he had had trouble wrapping them and had opened them several times afterwards to check to contents. There was an ink rubber and a packet of labels for John, a giant box of matches for Alan, a piece of purple bath soap for my mother, and a handkerchief with C on it for me. We were all very pleased with what we'd got.

Then there was the dinner. Mischa came, and Bobby, and the editor of the *Chronicle* and his wife, and some other friends. Tim was allowed to stay up because it was a fare-well party. There were champagne cocktails to start with, and Alan produced a special claret to go with the meal. We had turkey, because the parents wouldn't get that on their coral island, with roast potatoes and chestnut stuffing, brussels sprouts and cranberry sauce. Then there was one of Boney's famous home-made Christmas puddings, which are huge and very dark and so soaked in brandy that when Alan lights them they flame all over and burn for easily half a minute. Alan made a speech and Mischa repeated his story about Mrs Kawate and the fake Guarnerius that she had left him in her will. We laughed a lot and Tim got over-excited, although he'd only drunk coke, shouting in what he thought was a Japanese accent and falling dead on the floor the way Mrs Kawate had. We had some trouble getting him to bed.

We helped Boney clear up, John and I. Later, when the guests were settled in the living-room with liqueurs and port and cigars, we slipped out and walked a little way down the King's Road. The weather was damp and mild, unusual for December. The long-range forecast had promised us a cold Christmas, with ice and snow, but there was no sign of it so far.

'Look.' I nudged John as we turned back into Nelson Square. 'Those three men. They're the ones who are going to start the music boutique.'

Mr Yamaguchi and his friends were ahead of us. They got into their Honda and were driving away when we passed. John looked at them with interest.

'We three kings of Orient are,' he said. 'One in a bus and one in a car. One on a scooter, blowing his hooter –'

'They don't go by bus and they haven't got a scooter,' I pointed out.

'Pity,' said John. 'It spoils the song. How about Honda, rhymes with yonder? I'll have to work on it.'

The parents left the next day, the sixteenth. The three of us went to the airport in the car provided by the *Chronicle* to see them off. There was a press conference and drinks and sandwiches in a private room. Flash bulbs popped. Reporters pushed their way between us. The Firth-Beresford team was off again, in the usual blaze of publicity. In four days' time they would leave Cleveland Bay in the *Australian Princess*. By Christmas they would be settled in on their lonely island. A helicopter would lower their supplies. They'd be cut off from civilization for two months, with only a weekly radio link to keep them in touch with the outside world. We wouldn't see them again till February.

Bobby came back in the car with us.

'Lord,' she said. 'I hope they haven't forgotten anything.'

I don't know why she always said this when they went off. She was so efficient that she never let them leave anything behind. It was she who made all the arrangements for our Christmas, tickets, passports, dates, lists. Boney would be in charge on the spot, but Bobby was behind her for emergencies. The three of us appreciated this situation and we were used to it. After all, it wasn't the first time the parents had gone away.

It was colder that evening. And colder still the next day. Real winter was coming.

The winter of the violins.

*Is There a Doctor
in the House?*

I

Two days before we were due to fly to France Tim started
sniffing and coughing and it looked as if he'd caught a cold.
Boney ordered him to stay indoors. He argued for a while.
He'd been having a good time, riding his two-wheeler round
the square followed by envious neighbourhood children
who hadn't had their Christmas presents yet. But when
Boney pointed out that he wouldn't be popular in the aeroplane with a streaming cold, he gave in.

'I suppose I better.'

'That's a sensible boy,' said Boney. 'I tell you what, I'll
bring your tea upstairs on a nice little tray. You can have it
in bed. How about that?'

'O.K.,' said Tim. 'And I'll have Charlotte's radio and my
stamp book.'

He spent the afternoon in bed with the radio on full-blast.
He didn't seem very hungry at tea-time and his nose was
running terribly, but he didn't complain. John went up to
see him after we'd had our supper, to explain about stamp-
collecting in general and the particular specimens that were
already in the album. But when he got there Tim had turned
off his light and the radio and was fast asleep.

'Well, let's hope he sleeps it off,' said Boney. 'We'll be able
to tell in the morning, and if he's worse I'll get the doctor to
him. Goodnight all, and don't stay up too late with the
telly.'

She padded off down the stairs to her basement.

The next day when she came up to look at Tim he was

hot and flushed and spotty. She went downstairs at once to telephone the doctor. John and I wandered half-dressed in and out of Tim's room, not knowing what to do for the best. Tim was in despair.

'The spots are nothing!' he wailed hoarsely. 'I'm only too hot, that's all. Take away my temperature, Charlotte, then I'll be all right!'

He used to think that the thermometer was for cooling you down. I fetched it from the bathroom cupboard and managed to get it under his tongue. We all sat silent for one minute by John's watch, to give it a good chance.

'A hundred and four,' I announced as cheerfully as I could.

'Lucky man,' said John in a passable imitation of our doctor's bedside manner. 'You're going to spend a few days tucked up in bed. Keep him warm, plenty of liquids –'

Tim wept again.

'I can't stay in bed! I got to go to France tomorrow in the aeroplane! Waww-ww!'

'Well,' said John patiently. 'They don't allow spots in aeroplanes, Tim. They have this spot check. Any spots and they tell you to go home.'

'Waww-ww!'

'Come on ,don't cry. Perhaps the planes will be grounded anyway, because it's snowing. See?'

It had certainly got much colder overnight. It wasn't actually snowing, but there certainly was a little sleet drifting past Tim's window. He twisted on his pillow and gave it a disdainful stare.

'It's not real snow.'

'It will be soon,' insisted John. 'The weather report said London and the home counties, sleet or snow. And when it snows in London it really snows. The buses get stuck. And the planes skid on the runways and can't take off.'

'True?' Tim turned bloodshot eyes to me for confirmation.

'True. Don't you worry, Tim. We won't go tomorrow. We'll go another day.'

'Yes.' He sniffed horribly and cheered up. 'We'll go another day, when it's not snowing. And when the spots have gone.'

'That's right,' said John. 'We'd never get you through the customs as you are. They'd spot you at once.'

'Joke,' said Tim, smiling feebly.

'Doctor's coming to us first,' said Boney, bustling back upstairs with a box of paper tissues and a glass of orange juice. She was always at her best when anyone was ill, all action and good temper. 'There we are, old Tim. Blow your nose on these. I'll make your bed nicely, and tuck you up tight. How about a nice drink of juice?'

'Yes,' said Tim. 'And come back and stay with me. And Charlotte, ask Bobby for some new tickets, for another day. And leave the door open. And ask Mischa to come and see me. And when is my violin coming?'

'And get dressed, you two,' ordered Boney. 'We don't want the doctor coming and thinking this is the Garden of Eden. I'll get some breakfast going.'

Sitting round the breakfast table, we faced the fact that we'd have to change our plans.

'It's measles, if you ask me,' said Boney. 'He won't be able to go.'

'That's the end,' groaned John. 'I was just beginning to look forward to it.'

'You can go on your own if you like,' I pointed out. 'She's your aunt.'

'Great-aunt,' corrected John. 'And French. And only related by marriage.'

'I'm not leaving Tim,' I said. 'Not at Christmas.'

'Nor am I,' said Boney. 'I don't mind about Derby, not a

bit. Save my train fare. The old man can go to his sister's, and I'll stay here. Between you and me, her place is so cold I don't envy him. Which reminds me, I'd better get him to turn up the heating. Keep our Tim warm.'

'I'm staying too, then,' said John. 'My French is awful anyway. And I might be useful, fetching prescriptions. Shopping. Getting in the yule log.'

'Don't I wish I'd made a Christmas cake,' sighed Boney. 'I'll have to run up a quick one. And there'll have to be a dinner of some sort. You wait, we'll have a lovely time. Now Charlotte, you'd better cancel those plane reservations. And what about John's auntie?'

'Great-auntie,' said John.

'They've probably got a telephone,' I said. 'We'll try ringing up, and if that doesn't work we'll send a telegram. Regret beaucoup. Tiny Tim malade.'

2

'Lucky man,' said the doctor. 'You're going to spend a few days tucked up in bed. Keep warm, plenty of liquids –'

'That's what John said,' croaked Tim, smiling faintly.

'I'll come and see you tomorrow, Tim old boy. I'll listen to your nice spotty chest again with my listening machine.'

'Your stethoscope, you mean.'

'Yes. Clever old chap. Bye-bye.'

'Bye.' Tim turned on his side and sniffed sadly. He looked very miserable.

'Measles, of course,' said the doctor as we went downstairs. 'I'm afraid that means staying where he is for at least two weeks. You'll manage, won't you, Mrs Bowen?'

Boney, who had put on a clean white overall specially for his visit, swelled up even bigger than usual and looked as if she were matron at London's biggest hospital.

'Yes, Doctor. I think you can trust me, as I've seen the other two through it. John and Charlotte, they had the measles that April when the parents were in Canada.'

'So they did. You'll have to put off that trip to France, I'm afraid. Any relatives in London, Charlotte?'

'No, not really.' It was too complicated to explain that for one reason or another almost everybody we knew was going away for Christmas. 'But I'm going to telephone the Latour-Beresfords. They're related by marriage.'

'Good girl.'

'We'll manage,' said Boney firmly. 'And there's Bobby. Miss Robson that is.'

'Jolly good. I'll be in tomorrow. Weather's not too promising, is it?'

A little more sleet fell from a cold leaden sky.

'Je suis Charlotte, Charlotte Firth.' The line to France was terrible and I wasn't sure that I was speaking to Great-aunt Clothilde. John, at my side, sniggered and put me off. 'Buzz off,' I hissed.

'What do you say?' said the voice.

Ici Charlotte Firth. Mon frère Tim est malade –'

'Oui, oui, now I understand. You are Charlotte? I am Clothilde Latour-Beresford. Oh, he is sick, the Tim? Poor, poor.'

'I'm afraid we won't be able to come. We can't leave him, not at Christmas.'

'Naturally you cannot leave,' she agreed. 'You have some nurse in the house?'

'Well, no. There's Boney, I mean Mrs Bowen. She's looking after us.'

Far away in France Great-aunt Clothilde failed to comprehend. I had to say it again. Still she wasn't satisfied.

'I will fix,' she said. 'I do not know the bone you speak of. I will fix Madeleine to come to you. She is medicine, you understand. Student.'

'Yes, I see what you mean. But please don't bother her. We're all right really. Mrs Bowen will look after us.'

'Madeleine will come. She goes already from Edimbourg.'

'Please, I don't want to spoil her Christmas. We're all right, it's only measles, you know. Nothing serious. Red spots. Des choses rouges.'

'Oui, oui, I understand. Is sometimes dangereux. Also for the bone. I telephone immediately Madeleine. Au revoir!'

'But really we can manage –'

There was a sudden ear-shattering click. She'd rung off.

'What happened?' asked John. 'Is she furious?'

'No,' I said. 'I couldn't make her understand. She thinks we need help. She's sending Madeleine.'

John looked at me in dismay.

'Madeleine! But she's beastly, she's got red hair. She's a bully and half-French and she'll ruin everything. I mean, I don't mind staying here for Christmas, but not with some vile foreign woman coming in and ordering us about!'

'Well, I can't do anything about it, can I? Except ring up and cancel our reservations. Shut up until I've finished.'

We told Boney about Madeleine. She went cross and sniffy and said never in all her years with us had anyone inferred that she couldn't look after us properly.

'I'm sorry, Boney,' I said.

'The Latour-Beresfords are like that,' added John. 'You can't argue with them. Vile bullies.'

'She'd better go in the spare room,' said Boney, sighing heavily. 'Come on, Charlotte. Get the sheets and I'll help you make up the bed. When's she coming?'

Feeling foolish, I realized I didn't know.

'If she's coming from Edinburgh she can't be here before tomorrow,' said John. 'Tomorrow at the earliest.'

'Plenty of time,' said Boney, cheering up. 'I'll nip out and get in something nice. These Frenchies like their food. How about a joint for tomorrow, a nice bit of beef. And I'd better get a piece of ham. And plenty of veg, and fruit. I'll think about our Christmas dinner later.'

'Boney,' said John, his eyes lighting up. 'There's something I've always wanted to try, and that's goose. Please, please can we have goose? We may never get a chance again.'

'I'll think about it. One thing at a time.'

'Christmas is coming and the goose is getting fat,' insisted John. 'Please, Boney.'

'Goose, what next?' she said. 'Go on, take that up to Tim and I'll get something on the table for you two. Tell him I'll be up soon.'

'And we'd better get a tree,' shouted John from the stairs. 'I'll ask Mick. And some decorations and holly and mistletoe and lights – whoops! Nearly spilt it.'

'If he's upset my tray I'll be after him,' threatened Boney.

Miraculously John got to Tim's room without spilling anything, but it wasn't much good. Tim, flushed, hot and miserable, wasn't hungry.

Mischa came in at tea-time, expecting to find us ready to go the next day. We told him about Tim and the changed plans.

'He wants to see you,' I remembered. 'He wants to know when his violin is coming.'

'You better not go near him, Mischa,' said Boney. 'Not with your concerts and everything. I've heard of people having measles more than once, grown-ups too.'

Mischa thought about it and decided he'd risk going as far as the door. Tim was pleased to see him and managed to prop himself up on his elbow.

'Hallo Mischa. I have to stay in bed because of measles. I got spots.'

'Poor old Tim. Yes, I can see your spots from here. Get better soon, won't you.'

'I don't know,' said Tim. 'I don't know when I will. But I can't go to France. I got to stay here. When is that violin coming?'

'Oh yes. The violin. Today's Monday. Well, it's coming tomorrow, the twentieth, in a big crate with Mr Yamaguchi's violins. Boney will let them in and they'll put it in the studio. I'll open it when I get back from Birmingham.'

'When you going?'

'Tomorrow morning.'

'You just been there, haven't you?'

'Yes, we had a rehearsal. We'll have another tomorrow, midday, and then we'll play it properly in the evening. It's the Beethoven. Dah, dah, dah, di-di dah-h dah-h. You know.'

'Yes,' said Tim and sang the rest of the phrase. 'Who's going to be the conductor?'

'Mirmanov. He's very good.'

'When you coming back?'

'Wednesday. I can't come back tomorrow night. It will be too late, after the concert. I'll have to stay in a hotel.'

'I see,' said Tim. 'It's a pity, but I'll have to wait.'

'Yes, but not long, Tim. When I get back on Wednesday I'll open the big crate and we'll get the violin out and have a look at it.'

'And it might be what Mrs Kawate said?'

'It might. A Guarnerius. Probably not.'

'She ray down and die,' remembered Tim, smiling faintly. He lay down himself and waved a hot hand. 'Bye.'

'Bye Tim. You'll be much better by Wednesday and we'll have fun with that violin. Bye.'

As we went downstairs together I asked Mischa where he was going for Christmas. Then I remembered Sandy Lovelace and wished I hadn't. He'd spent last Christmas with her and her parents in the country.

'I've got no plans, Char. Mischa Lewis the well-known concert violinist is spending Christmas quietly in his London studio. As you're staying, perhaps we can join up?'

We put it to Boney and she was delighted. She said it would make the day for her, Frenchwoman or no Frenchwoman. She'd pack the old man off to his sister's and we'd have a lovely party of our own.

'Goose,' said John. 'Please.'

'Oh John, you do go on so,' said Boney. 'Now look, a goose is a great big bird, enough for ten people, and there's only going to be the five of us, and Tim upstairs. He won't want much, not the way he's looking. I tell you what though. I might get a duck. It's ever so good with orange sauce.'

John's eyes sparkled greedily. 'Mmmm. That sounds all right. What for pudding?'

'Well, you've had your Christmas one, haven't you. So I might make meringues, with nuts and cream, or ice-cream, or frozen raspberries. I'll think about it.'

'Boney, you're a Christmas angel! Let me help you to fly!' John got his arms around her and with a huge effort lifted her off the ground, but she was so heavy that he had to let her down even before she shrieked.

'Enough! You'll be the death of me!' She blushed and smoothed down her skirt. 'Just give me a bit of peace.'

Mischa helpfully offered to take John to the King's Road

57

Odeon to see *Assignment*, a new thriller which had just been released, and Boney said I must go too and she would leave her door open and listen for Tim. It was not really my sort of film, dead bodies and blood and fast cars and girls. But John loved it and so did Mischa. Mischa said it was the best he'd seen. He always liked murder stories and films with violence in them, which was surprising because he was a very unviolent person. He said they were a good form of relaxation, which he needed particularly just then as he'd started work on a major project. As well as his preparation for concerts and recitals he was working on the whole series of Bach partitas and chaconnes, so that he could include them in his repertoire.

It was very cold coming home that night, and we went as fast as we could, clutching our coats, trying to hold in the last of the Odeon's stuffy warmth. Sleet lay thinly in the little garden in the middle of Nelson Square.

'She telephoned,' said Boney, as we burst frozen-faced into the hall. 'The French lady. She sounded quite nice, I thought. Ever so friendly and doesn't want to step on my toes. Maybe it won't be too bad. Your supper's in the kitchen, and there's plenty for you too, Mischa. Go on, you're all skin and bone. You don't eat half enough.'

Mischa was persuaded.

'I suppose she's coming on the night train,' said John. 'The demoiselle Française avec les cheveux rouges.'

'I don't know about rouge,' said Boney, 'but she said she'd be here in the morning. It was ever such a bad line. It's a long way off, Scotland. And Tim's all right, Charlotte. He woke up once and I gave him a drink and aspirin. Goodnight all.'

Mischa went soon after we'd eaten and cleared up. He was fussy about early nights before concerts.

'See you Wednesday,' he said, collecting his coat and making for the broom cupboard. 'Thanks for the supper.'

We thanked him for *Assignment*.

'Play well,' said John. 'Show Birmingham how it's done.'

'Thanks. Goodnight. Goodnight, Char.'

'Goodnight Mischa. Good luck.'

He went, stooping among the brooms, his thick black hair brushing the cupboard ceiling.

'I've got him a super Christmas present,' I told John.

'What?'

'It's a black silk scarf, Victorian, with a long fringe. I got it in the Antique Market.'

'Perfect. He can wear it with his concert overcoat.'

The concert overcoat was a big heavy black one with an astrakhan collar, second-hand like the scarf I'd got for him.

'I've made him an ashtray,' said John.

'He doesn't smoke.'

'Well, never mind. He'll use it for something. Old strings. Resin. Used concert tickets. It's the shape of a violin. Quite difficult to make.'

'Can't wait to see it,' I said, putting out the lights.

On the way up to bed we stopped on the dark landing and looked down into the square.

'There's snow coming,' said John, pressing his nose to the cold window-pane. 'You get a feeling of everything standing still, waiting for it. It gets colder and colder, and you wait, and then it comes. Hallo, there's our friend.'

'Which friend?'

'You know. Miaow. What's-his-name?'

'Lee.'

'Yes. That's his Bentley.'

The big car turned silently at our end of the square, drove past us and back towards the King's Road. We couldn't see

59

inside. And it might have been anyone's car, as I pointed out. There are lots of Bentleys around.

Up in my room on the top floor I unpacked the suitcase which had been waiting there for tomorrow. I hung the Christmas dress in the cupboard with the birthday coat. I wouldn't be needing them. Tomorrow was the twentieth, the day on which we should have caught the plane to Paris with Madeleine Latour-Beresford and gone on with her to the château for Christmas and boar-hunting. Now everything was changed. Madeleine, described by John as a red-haired beast, was coming to London instead and we were going to have an odd makeshift Christmas in London with no parents and a sick spotty Tim.

Tomorrow I would telephone some friends and see who was going to be in London. I might even telephone Graham. He would be back from Leeds by now. I might. But on the other hand I couldn't. He hadn't written or sent a Christmas card. He didn't want to hear from me.

And that reminded me, I hadn't heard from Cambridge about my exam. Which probably meant I hadn't got a place.

I sat on the edge of my bed feeling gloomy. Prospects for Christmas were not good.

And then I remembered, suddenly. Presents! Those other presents which we hadn't opened with the parents, hidden somewhere for after France. Boney would know where. We'd have them for our private Christmas. All those surprises from friends and relations, socks, handkerchiefs, chocolates, toys, beautiful coffee-table books. Those expensive things from people on the *Chronicle* for all the family. And there was my present for Boney, all wrapped for me to give to her before I left. It was a book called *You and Your Stars* and it told you how to read your own horoscope. And the black silk scarf for Mischa. And talking of the

Chronicle, I must telephone Bobby tomorrow and tell her what was happening.

I could hear John below, singing in the bath. I went down and shouted at him through the keyhole.

'Get out, can't you! You've been in there half an hour!'

'All right, all right!' he shouted back. 'When I don't have a bath you say I'm dirty and when I do you tell me to get out!'

'I was thinking,' I called, leaning on the door. 'We'd better get busy tomorrow and get that tree and decorations and things. And I'll telephone Bobby and perhaps she'll come round –'

John was out of the bath by now and he suddenly opened the door and I tumbled in at his feet. He thought I was very funny.

3

The twentieth.

Looking back I remember it as a day of activity, people coming and going, parcels arriving, friends telephoning, excitement in the air. Something made me wake up early. I got up at eight, all energy and good resolutions. I gave myself a health breakfast of black coffee, yoghurt and an apple, planning to get so slim and beautiful that Graham, if he ever came back, wouldn't recognize me. I made a list of people to telephone and another of things to do.

Outside in the square Mischa, wearing the concert overcoat and his fur gloves and fur hat, was getting into a taxi.

The Admiral, walking Skipper, helped him in with his violin case and a small overnight bag. I waved from the front window. Off to Birmingham. Back tomorrow.

The Admiral rang our doorbell as soon as Mischa had gone.

'Sorry about Tim,' he said. 'Bad show. I gather you've had to postpone the invasion of France. Let me know if there's anything I can do. Come on, Skipper.'

I'd hardly thanked him and said goodbye when the bell rang again. Mick stood on the steps, padded out with so many woollies that his coat would hardly button up.

'Here you are then,' he said. 'The missus told me to bring this along for Tim. And the tree is off the barrow, with compliments of the season.' He held out a large flimsy aeroplane, and a Christmas treet neatly furled like an umbrella. 'It don't fly, but the tree's all right. Just cut the strings and let it stand. Cold, innit? I'm going to pack it in if this goes on. Cor.'

The sleet was turning to snow, enough to lie white and sludgy in the street. Fred the milkman pulled his truck to a standstill, leaving furrows behind him.

'You could have knocked me down with a fevver,' he said, blowing warm breath into ice-cold air. 'Your Tim with the measles. Life's not all roses, eh? Just you tell him though, when he comes out on the pavement again I'll be waiting for him same as ever. Once a friend always a friend. Isn't that so, sweetheart?'

Geraldine hunched her shoulders and stamped her feet.

'My, that poor kid,' she said. 'I just hope he gets better soon. You having Christmas here then?'

I stood on the doorstep with the front door open, warm house behind me, dead cold outside. John appeared in a dressing-gown.

'It'll be a good Christmas,' I told Geraldine. 'Just us and Boney and Mischa. We'll have fun.'

'We might have a duck,' added John.

'Mischa doesn't want milk today, does he?' asked Fred.

'No thanks. He's staying the night in Birmingham. He won't be back till lunch-time tomorrow.'

'That bad Honda,' said Geraldine. 'There he is. Don't let me catch him parking in this square.'

Mr Yamaguchi and his friends drove round the square rather too fast, skidding in the thin slush, and out into the King's Road again, just as the doctor drove in at the other side and double-parked next to Fred's truck.

'How about shutting that door?' cried Boney, bustling out from the kitchen. 'What do you think we're doing, trying to central-heat the whole square? Oh good morning Doctor, I didn't know it was you.'

'Quite a reception committee.' The doctor nodded at the group assembled on our doorstep. 'How's my patient?'

We took him upstairs to see Tim. John was sent to his room to get dressed or else.

Tim was very quiet that morning, red in the face, short of breath. He lay limp, watching the small snowflakes falling past his window, while the doctor examined him thoroughly, listened to his chest, prodded his stomach, inspected his ears. The usual bedside chat seemed to have dried up.

'That's fine, Tim.' He folded his stethoscope and put it away in his bag. 'I'll come and see you tomorrow. Soon have you right.'

'Real snow,' said Tim. 'So the aeroplanes can't take off. But I've got this one.' He pointed to Mick's present, parked on his pillow.

'That's right. Perhaps we'll have a white Christmas. You eat any breakfast?'

'No. Juice.'

'Never mind. You'll feel better tomorrow. Goodbye.'

Measles bring complications from time to time, he told us on the way down. No bright lights, no straining the eyes. Warmth. Quiet. Nothing to worry about so far, but we shouldn't hesitate to telephone him.

'I'll go out shopping right now,' said Boney when she'd seen him off. 'Before the shops get too crowded. Tell John to hurry up and get these things from Mick, off this list. There. And you ring Bobby, Charlotte, like you said. Poor old Tim, he looks rotten doesn't he. Take this drink up, will you. And tell him I'll be back in twenty minutes. We'll have him right in a day or two.'

I did all the things she told me, hustled John, took Tim his drink and telephoned Bobby.

'Lord,' she said when she heard my voice. 'You've missed the plane.'

I explained.

'Lord,' she said again. 'I think I'd better come round now and see if there's anything I can do.'

'We're all right. A relation is coming, and Boney is a wonderful nurse.'

'I'm coming all the same. I'll collect those tickets off you, and I might do some Christmas shopping. Is it snowing like mad down the King's Road?'

'Yes.'

'I'll get there somehow, even if I have to hire a sledge.'

Real snow. Yesterday's fine sleet had fallen fast, like rain. This was different. The bigger the flakes the slower they fell. They danced this way and that, swirling away upwards as if unwilling to land, then floating down to settle like feathers on black pavements and grimy streets.

Eleven o'clock. John returned triumphant from Mick's barrow. He'd had to make two trips. Carrots, potatoes, sprouts, chestnuts, celery, tangerines, walnuts, onions, red cabbage, holly and mistletoe mounted up in the hall. He stood in the open doorway stamping the snow off his feet and beating it off his head and shoulders.

'Poor old Tim,' he said. 'He'd love to be out in this. It's a real blizzard.'

'Hurry up. You're letting a lot of cold air in.'

Snowflakes jogged our vision. They were coming so thick now that we could hardly see across the square. A lone motor-bike pottered down the far side, engine noise muffled by the snow, stopping at one door, then another. Then it moved jerkily on and round the corner towards us, black outlines blurred with white, like the picture on a faulty television set. Coming into better focus, it drew into the kerb by our house. The rider dismounted, hitched the big heavy thing on its stand, and came up to the door. Black leather coat, leggings, goggles, scarf and a helmet with a peak had all collected a lot of snow.

'Do you want twenty-three?' asked John, making as if to shut the door on this abominable snowman, who was stamping feet on our doorstep and scattering snow on our mat.

A mumbled reply through the scarf. Gloves were pulled off, revealing small thin hands, blue with cold. Small black boots below bulging leggings, caked with snow. Goggles off, showing brown eyes, red-rimmed with cold, but sparkling in the middle. Nose very pink. Peaked helmet off. Lumps of snow falling about us. Long bright red hair. A friendly smile.

Rudely we stood and stared. It must be the Frenchwoman, the dreaded red-haired beast. It couldn't be anyone else.

'I'm Madeleine.' She gave me frozen fingers to shake.

'Oh yes, sorry, of course. I'm Charlotte Firth. And this is John. Please come in. You must be terribly cold.'

'Understatement of the year,' she said. Hardly a trace of a French accent. She divested herself of coat, leggings and several other layers, gradually peeling down to sweater and jeans. She was a small, red-haired beast, rather skinny. John goggled, speechless. I had to nudge him when she asked if he'd be kind enough to fetch her suitcase off the back of the bike.

'Oh. Right. O.K.,' he gulped, and slithered down the steps to oblige, lingering to admire the great heavy machine, the wide handlebars, generous petrol tank, fat pedals, chromium levers, sturdy wheels, all now partly draped in snow.

'Come on, John. We're getting cold!'

'I'll show him the bike later,' said Madeleine, pushing the red hair back over her shoulders.

We got the door shut and both started talking at once and had to keep apologizing so that the other could get a word in.

'I thought you'd come to the wrong house –'

'I knew you were Charlotte, but I would never have recognized John –'

'There's Tim too, he's up in bed. Sorry? Yes, the doctor's been, he says –'

'Oh thanks, John. Sorry, where shall I put these?'

'Mrs Bowen, we call her Boney, but she's very fat. I tried to explain to your mother –'

'I'm a medical student, did you know? Sorry. Oh no, I'm fine. Gosh, your house is lovely and warm. My digs in Edinburgh –'

'The Bowens live in the basement and her old man, that's her husband, is going to Derby for Christmas, but Boney's staying –'

'I'd much rather be here than at the château. Mama's Christmas is very formal –'

John timidly asked how many miles the bike did to the gallon.

'Oh about sixty,' said Madeleine casually.

We hung her clothes in the airing-cupboard and started upstairs towards Tim and the spare room. John trailed after us, gaping with amazement.

'I can't believe it,' he muttered.

'What?'

'I mean, all the way from Edinburgh on that bike. It's – it's impossible. Even for a man –'

'Oh gosh no,' said Madeleine. 'I was staying with some people in Highgate. I came down from Edinburgh days ago, by train. The bike is just borrowed for the holidays.'

John still couldn't get over it.

'Well, even from Highgate it isn't bad. In a blizzard.'

We took her to see Tim, who was deeply impressed, and then I heard Boney coming in. I went down to meet her and Madeleine followed.

'Boney, this is her. Madeleine.'

They shook hands.

'Pleased to meet you I'm sure, Miss,' said Boney, not too friendly, easing off the vast Air Force greatcoat which she'd bought in the surplus stores. 'I'll get on with my work, if you'll excuse me.'

She smoothed her tartan skirt, pulled her hand-knitted sweater firmly down over her big hips, and reached for her apron.

'Please call me Madeleine,' said Madeleine. She eyed the sweater. 'That's lovely. Did you knit it yourself?'

Boney thawed slight. 'I did actually. Like it?'

'Gosh yes. It's beautifully finished. Actually I've brought some knitting with me and I've made a mistake about twenty rows down. I'll have to unpick it some time –'

'You better let me have a look at it,' said Boney. 'I don't mind unpicking. I'll soon get it straightened out. You got the pattern, Miss? I mean Madeleine.'

They were off. I went away to the telephone and arranged

to meet two schoolfriends in the King's Road for shopping that afternoon. When Boney discovered that Madeleine was a medical student their friendship was sealed. They began to talk illnesses and continued non-stop for the rest of the morning. Snatches of conversation drifted out of the kitchen, where they were busy peeling potatoes together.

'They opened her up because the surgeon thought it was gallstones, but when they got inside –'

'You should have seen, Boney! Poor man, his face was so swollen –'

'And I said to my sister-in-law : "If you don't see a doctor you're going to be sorry," but she wouldn't listen –'

'They say it can be terribly painful –'

'They used to put compresses on it –'

'They said she would probably have twins –'

'Might have lost an eye –'

'Had to have his wisdom teeth out –'

Then Bobby came, her arms full of parcels, most of which seemed to be presents for us.

'Here,' she said, thrusting the biggest ones into my arms. 'Lord, it's nothing. What sort of a Christmas are you going to have, you poor benighted infants?'

'Wonderful,' said John. 'Madeleine's here and she came on a huge bike and she's rather super. Except she and Boney won't stop talking.'

Later my friends came. Snow lay thick in the square. Like polar explorers we struggled out together to the King's Road, where crisp white was churned into slushy brown by passing buses and cars. There were crowds in the shops and far too many lovely things to buy. We spent our money and came back home for a record session in my room. Blues were my favourite that year. We shut John out, and he was vexed and sat moping outside on the landing, complaining that he had nothing to do. Tactfully Madeleine asked if he would take her down to Bowens' basement where she was introduced to the old man, who was just leaving for his sister's in Derby with a battered suitcase and a string-bag full of Christmas parcels. Then she went upstairs and read Tim a story. To please her he sat up and ate some tea.

'Never mind that bike,' said Geraldine generously, making her last round of the day. 'Just you put a note on it saying Number Twenty-three. Then I come by. I ring the bell. I say When you going to move this bike? And you say I move it right now, Warden. You see now?'

'Gosh. That's kind of you,' said Madeleine.

'And how's that kid?' asked Geraldine. 'My, I hope he get better soon.'

And at some point during the afternoon a van came with the crate which Mischa was expecting. Mr Yamaguchi's violins and Mrs Kawate's fake Guarnerius from Japan. I didn't see the van. I was upstairs with my friends. John said, afterwards, that it was a Bedford, painted yellow. It had Oriental Freight painted on the side. It looked as if it had been done recently. The letters were very bright, although the van was not a new model. It was difficult to be sure because it was getting dark.

John and Boney opened Mischa's front door and helped the driver manhandle the crate down the passage and into the studio. He was a friendly rat-faced man, strong in the shoulders, wearing a brown woolly cap on his small neat head. Boney offered him a cup of tea and took him through the broom cupboard to the kitchen.

'Many thanks,' he said when he'd finished. 'Must go. Got to put the van away before bad light stops play. Busy day for yours truly.'

M.V. – 4

Boney thought he was quite a character. He smelt rather of stale tobacco, but was otherwise inoffensive.

We had a very cosy supper, Boney, Madeleine, John and I.

'I think Mischa Lewis is one of the best young violinists in England today,' said Madeleine.

'Have you met him?' asked John.

'No, but I've heard him play. In Edinburgh, and Dundee. And once in Newcastle.'

'You'll meet him tomorrow,' I told her. 'And he's having Christmas with us.'

'Tomorrow is the shortest day,' said John. 'Midwinter.'

Afterwards Boney attacked Madeleine's knitting and we watched television and went late to bed. We felt happy and secure in our warm house, with Boney in the basement and Madeleine in the spare room, and Tim getting better.

Outside it was cold and dim. The snow had stopped during the afternoon, and now it lay piled high, on the bike and on the cars in the square, and on roofs, balconies and window-ledges. Bare trees sprouted clusters of it, like white blossom. The pavements sparkled under the street lamps.

It was very pretty, like a Christmas card.

4

In Birmingham it was cold but not snowing. Mischa gave a fine performance of the Beethoven and Mirmanov congratulated him. Would he by any chance like a lift back to London? Mirmanov was conducting in Zurich the following evening and had to catch an early-morning plane from Heathrow. He had a chauffeur-driven Austin Princess waiting for him. Would enjoy Mischa's company.

Mischa thought a moment and accepted. He remembered the Bach he was working on, and poor sick Tim and Mrs Kawate's violin. He would be back sooner to start practising and open the crate. He cancelled his hotel room and set off with the conductor in the big comfortable car.

Snow met them halfway down the M1. Visibility was very bad. They slowed down and proceeded at snail's pace. Further on there was an hour-long delay where twelve vehicles had ploughed into one another and piled up, blocking the southbound carriageway. Mirmanov and Mischa dozed in the back of the car. It wasn't a very pleasant journey. The chauffeur was patient but weary. It was three in the morning by the time they reached Marble Arch.

Mirmanov was staying at a hotel in Park Lane. They dropped him at the door. Mischa and the chauffeur chatted as they went south to Sloane Square and along the King's Road. Nelson Square looked too snowy for the big heavy car. The chauffeur dropped him at the corner and went on home to Streatham, where he lived.

Snow lay deep, muffling all sound. As Mischa plodded sleepily home with his violin and his overnight bag, it began to snow again. It was dark at the bottom of the square, round the corner away from the last street lamp. He shuffled towards the studio, wondering if he should allow himself an extra hour in bed in the morning as he'd been up so late. He'd got a lot to do to that last partita. Nothing like ready yet. Complex and brainy music, only beautiful if played perfectly. Then he thought about the Beethoven, running through certain passages in his mind, re-playing to himself the end of the second movement and the opening of the *rondo*. He knew he'd played it well. The phrasing had satisfied him, and the pace. But wasn't there something else?

It was very late and Mischa was tired, but already he was thinking with pleasure of tomorrow's practising, and of re-learning the Beethoven one day, picking it to pieces, re-building it. Yes, that was it. He remembered his teacher in Paris saying to him : 'You wish to be a concert violinist, yes. Then all your life you will be a student.'

He smiled to himself as he took off one glove, put it in his pocket, and found his key.

He put the key in the lock and opened his front door.

As he groped for the light switch he sensed that something was wrong. Voices. Whispering. Movement in the studio. And someone put a soft hand over his mouth.

'Mischa, go! Please go, run away!'

He felt her fur. He knew her scent. Sandy. She tried to push him back, he struggled to get further in.

'Sandy! What the hell –'

The studio door was open. There was torchlight. He saw for an instant the open crate, men carrying violin cases, drawing more of them out from among paper wrappings and wood-shavings, like some crazy band collecting their instruments. Someone lying still on the floor, recognizable, sallow-faced, craning his neck towards the door in an attitude of despair.

Yamaguchi. Dead.

Mischa drew one breath, seeing, pausing on his own door-step. Then someone rushed at him, someone big and bulky. Hard metal struck his head. Blood ran down his face. Gasping, he clutched Sandy, trying to pull her outside into Lot's Passage and safety. She went limp in his arms. And then his own knees crumpled, he staggered and fell in the doorway. Just conscious, he felt the final blow, some vicious kick in the shin, but more than a kick. Something which snapped bone, swamped him with pain, kept him lying helpless.

Unconscious. Conscious, vaguely. Voices hissing above him. A fat face, slit-eyed.

'*Get rid of him!*'

Then nothing. No Sandy. Silence. Forgetfulness. Black oblivion blotted out everything, all memory and sensation, the sound of his music, the movement of the Austin Princess down the M1, the short walk down the deserted square, the shock, the pain.

Snow was falling, snow on snow.

The Shortest Day
the Longest Nightmare

I

'Tim?'

Waking out of deep sleep, I knew I'd heard him. I'd left my door open on purpose, in case he woke. I put on my bed-side light, left my blissful warm bed, and stumbled down-stairs to the first floor landing.

'Tim, don't cry. What's the matter?'

After years of being an older sister all this was completely automatic. He was on his way back from the bathroom and must have lost his way in the dark. He'd reached the top of the stairs instead of his bedroom door and was standing there sobbing miserably. I picked him up and carried him back to his room. His face was still hot and flushed, but he was shaking all over.

'I went downstairs,' he muttered through chattering teeth. 'I wanted to see my violin. But I was frightened.'

'Poor old Tim, you've had one of your bad dreams.' I tidied his bed, helped him in and tucked him up.

'C-cold.'

'There. You'll be all right in a minute. Your bed got cold while you were out. There.'

He tossed from side to side, still shuddering. 'I saw Mischa coming and then I couldn't sleep and I went down to the cupboard. I was frightened.'

A pattering of feet across the landing and Madeleine appeared, red hair in wild disorder. She took a quick look at him.

'I'll get the doctor,' she said in a low voice. 'Where's his number? Fetch another blanket. And a hot-water bottle. Quick as you can.'

I glanced at the kitchen clock while I waited for the kettle to boil. Five to four. Madeleine was telephoning in the study. We met going upstairs again.

'He's coming,' she whispered. 'It's probably pneumonia.'

I nodded. In a sleepy way I was wondering what I would have done if she hadn't been there. I tried to pull myself together.

'Here.' I gave her the hot-water bottle. 'You take this. I'll go and let him in.'

I went down again and waited in the sitting-room, holding the curtain back and peering out into the square. More snow, big soft flakes. Everything quiet and ghostly. There was the doctor now, on foot, hurrying along in the middle of the road where the snow wasn't lying so deep. He must have decided that his car would be more trouble than it was worth. He lived very near.

'Glad you called me,' he said, wide-awake, cheerful, taking off a thick scarf which revealed some bare chest and a half-buttoned pyjama jacket. 'Can't be too careful. Let's have a look, shall we.'

I sat yawning and nodding on the landing until he was finished. From behind Tim's closed door came muffled sounds. Crying. Moaning. Then Madeleine taking the doctor downstairs, their smooth professional talk mumbling below. The front door closing softly. Madeleine coming up the creaky bit of the stairs, probably on tiptoe. She needn't have worried because John was such a heavy sleeper that nothing would wake him short of a thunderstorm, and Boney was miles away in the basement with the door closed.

'All right?'

'Virus pneumonia,' she said.

'Oh no. Poor Tim. It's serious, isn't it. I'd better stay with him. I'll sleep on his sofa.'

'I will. You go back to bed. I'll call you if there's anything.'

'Promise?'

'Yes. Go on. He'll be all right. He's having an antibiotic. It's easy these days.'

Gratefully I went upstairs, crawled back into bed and dropped again into the lovely warm unconscious world I'd come from.

2

A long time later, so long that it seemed to him that the past was another lifetime, Mischa opened his eyes and stirred, painfully, knowing that he was badly hurt, lying somewhere dim and cold. Someone was moving about. Torchlight. A smell of damp, and stale tobacco, and paraffin. And another smell, which reminded him of laboratories, or hospitals. Anaesthetic.

He lay in a narrow bed which seemed to rock gently from side to side. He put out a hand to steady it, bracing himself against the hard wooden edge. Pain shot through him. The right leg. His head was throbbing and he felt sick. With difficulty he leaned out of his bed, where some kind person had thoughtfully put a plastic basin for him, retched feebly, and felt better.

Anaesthetic. Makes you sick.

'All right matey.'

The kind person, very close to him, smelling so strongly of

stale tobacco, laid him back on the hard mattress. I should thank him, thought Mischa. He's so kind. But the words wouldn't come. Just a wretched groan.

'Not too much noise, matey. I'll soon have you comfortable.'

In dim light a narrow clean-shaven face peered down, not unfriendly, like some eager small animal. A rat, or a weasel. Sharp nose. Bright eyes. A small neat head in a brown woolly cap. Big shoulders, surprising with that little ratty face. Firm hands, pulling covers over Mischa to keep him warm.

'Thank you. Very kind.'

He'd found the words at last. After that effort he lay still for a long time. His sharp-nosed rat-faced friend took the torch and moved away. The darkness was quiet and comforting. His bed rocked. Consciousness ebbed and flowed.

With an effort he thought back and tried to remember. There were strangers in the studio. That man on the floor was Yamaguchi, though. That he knew for sure. The strangers were pulling violins out of the crate. Why were they doing that? And Sandy, why was she there?

There must have been something they wanted. They wanted it badly. They couldn't wait for him to come back.

And then when he arrived they coshed him. He wasn't wanted, that was clear. They didn't want him in the studio.

Where am I now?

Very cautiously he turned his aching head and looked about him. He was in a small confined place with a low ceiling. Kind rat-face with his back turned was lighting a spill from the flame of a small paraffin heater. The heater had a friendly familiar look. So did the blue kettle which stood on the stove. He heard the hiss of gas. And beyond, outside in the darkness, the noise of water lapping softly on wood.

A boat.

Of course. That would account for the rocking. A boat

with a blue kettle. The smell of mud and ooze prevailing as the smell of anaesthetic died away.

The Thames.

Memories rushed back, from a lifetime ago. The summer and Sandy. The houseboat. The mermaid-prowed blue boat tethered furthest from the Embankment, its neighbour a derelict barge. Boiling water in the blue kettle. Making coffee. Cooking on that little stove in the galley, just the two of them. Then later, that day when he'd arrived unexpectedly and found a boy sitting here, on this bunk where he lay now, a drug addict, injecting himself. 'Just a friend,' Sandy had said. 'You don't understand.'

He lay back and closed his eyes. Nothing made sense. Sandy had been there in the studio. She had tried to warn him. Her soft hand, the fur and her scent. 'Mischa, go! Please go, run away!' She had been there, and then they had struck him down. Now he lay battered in her houseboat, dazed and sick. Pain almost everywhere, all over his body.

A nightmare.

His head ached. He put his hand up and felt a thick bandage. His vision was blurred by something sticking to his eyelashes. Probably blood. His right hip was very sore. And the right leg swamped him with surges of pain. He ran his hand cautiously towards it, jolted it slightly and winced. His trouser-leg was torn and rolled up above his knee to make room for splints. He could feel them. Gingerly he put his hand inside his jacket and felt his ribs. They hurt when he breathed. Both his feet were cold and numb. No shoes on. Just damp socks. His concert overcoat was spread over him as well as some other covers which smelt of damp.

His precious hands. Anxiously he felt them all over, rubbing them together, flexing the strong supple fingers. Cold, but in working order. That mattered more than anything else. Arms stiff, bruised, but moving. That was good too.

Another groan, relief this time, came pushing feebly through his lips.

'There, there,' said his friend, coming close. 'How about this then? It's the best yours truly could do. Got to improvise.' He pushed a plastic bottle gently under the covers near Mischa's feet. It was warm. He must have filled it from the kettle. 'Get your face washed next. Then we'll have a cuppa.'

'And get a doctor,' said Mischa. 'Must get a doctor.'

'Sorry matey.' The little face came close. 'I'm afraid that's out of the question. There's been a bit of trouble. So yours truly has to lie low. See what I mean?'

He lifted his hand into the torchlight. He was holding a gun.

Mischa looked at it for a long time, silent, blinking. He realized he'd never seen a gun before, not in all his curious sheltered musician's life. Familiar in films. Now here, a few inches from his face. A real gun.

He felt weak and cold.

'I see what you mean,' he said at last. 'Who are you?'

'Well, let's not worry about that.' Gun-toting rat-face pushed back his woolly cap and scratched his head. 'Tell you what. Call me Nurse. Yours truly prefers to remain anonymous. It's like this, matey. You arrived unexpected. They coshed you and beat you up, didn't they. Put the boot in. They thought you was dead, matey. And the boss said to get rid of you. But I didn't, did I.'

'Why?'

'Matey, we'll come to that. I got you in the back of the van, didn't I. Going to dump you in a place I know. You was unconscious. You knowed nothing. I looked at you. I said to myself, he's still breathing. So what do I do next?'

'I don't know,' said Mischa.

'Half a mo,' said Nurse. He went round the corner, out of

sight. Mischa remembered the lavatory there, small and cramped, tucked into the bows of the boat. Nurse was exploring with the torch. He came back balancing a soap-dish of water, the torch under his arm, a packet of cotton wool in the other hand. He'd put the gun away, somewhere, to Mischa's relief. His side pocket bulged. It was probably there. 'Let's clean you up a bit. Beauty treatment. It's all included in the price.'

The hands were expert. Surprisingly, Mischa found he trusted Nurse. He lay still under the dabbing cotton wool. Little rivulets of icy water dribbled down the side of his face and Nurse caught them deftly with quick swipes, frowning and muttering.

'Mmmm. Very nice. There. You might have to have a couple of stitches in the head later on. Nothing much else. Bumps and bruises. And your leg, of course. Simple fracture of the tibia, matey. I've set it to the best of my ability, which is quite something. Immobilised, in splints, see? I used my own medical supplies what I always carry for away matches. Luck day for you, matey. Sorry about the trousers. Your best suit, is it? Wear it for concerts? Well, they may be able to mend it. I tried to cut along the seam, matey. Not easy. Not the best-equipped operating-theatre in the world.'

'Ouch.' Nurse had found a cut on Mischa's cheek-bone.

'Go on, I'm not hurting you. As I was saying, you was still breathing. Now, I never killed a man, matey. You believe me. I patched up lots of them. That's my job. I patch them up. I said to myself one good turn deserves another. I patch him up and maybe he'll do me a favour. See what I mean?'

'Yes, Nurse,' said Mischa doubtfully.

Nurse swept his dirty swabs into the soap-dish and took it away. He came back with Sandy's first-aid kit. 'Not much in here,' he grumbled, picking over the miniature dressings.

'Make do with one of these. There. Beautiful as the day. Well, as I was saying. You lay blotto. Nobody around, only the weather. I turned the van and brought her down this side, by the steps. Know where I mean?'

'Yes. Opposite the barge.'

'Yes. I got my ether and I give you a whiff now and again for the sake of peace and quiet. I lay you on an old sack and pull you along like a sledge, see. All along the barge. It's covered with snow, and a little still coming down. Then I carried you aboard here and got you below.'

'I don't know how you did it, Nurse. I'm heavy.'

'You're nothing, matey. I've been a weightlifter in my time. You were blotto. You didn't give trouble. I got the leg fixed to my satisfaction. Then I had to go back and move the van, didn't I. Back to its cosy garage. It'll be painted back its old colour by now. The boss never forgets the artistic details. You got to admire him for that. Then I come back here to my patient. I tell you, it's been a busy day for yours truly. Looking forward to a bit of shut-eye.'

'What was going on, Nurse, I mean in my studio –'

'Half a mo. Kettle's boiling. We'll have that cuppa. Since the milkman hasn't yet called we'll have to have it without.'

Nurse smiled at his own joke as he bustled about in the galley. Mischa lay silent. The boss had said 'Get rid of him.' He'd heard that. But Nurse, for reasons unknown, had spirited him away and was making him a cup of tea.

He recognized the mug. In the summer, two mugs, one for him and one for Sandy. Nurse lifted his head and he sipped gratefully at the dark sweet liquid.

'Drink up. Do you good. I'd put a spot of rum in it for you, but you're not supposed to with a head wound.'

'What were they doing?' asked Mischa, between sips. 'What was going on?'

'I might as well tell you, matey. The Japanese captain

brought a consignment in, all packed in them violin cases. Beautifully done it was. He used your place to avoid suspicion. Then the boss did a deal with him. Half and half. Provided the van and the moral support, see what I mean. But the Jap got a bit uppity. Wanted a bigger share. So the boss had to arrange a little burglary, didn't he.'

'Who's the boss, Nurse? Who is he?'

'No names, no pack drill, matey. He just didn't want anybody on his pitch, that's all. The Jap followed us there, came busting in at the last moment. There was a spot of trouble, see.'

Mischa's head felt congested with thoughts. It throbbed and heaved. He closed his eyes to think better.

'You said a consignment, in the violin cases. What of?'

'Snow, matey. We were going to store it here, in the boat. But there's been a change of plan. Unforeseen circumstances. It's going straight on the market.'

'Snow?'

'Yes, snow. You never heard that expression, matey? Snow. Horse. Heroin.'

'No,' said Mischa. His voice sounded very small. 'No. I never heard it called that.'

'Snow. The hard stuff. The heavy roller,' went on Nurse. 'It's all the same thing. Not that I approve of drugs, matey. Except for medical purposes. More trouble than they're worth. The boss only came in because the Jap brought the consignment right to his front door, you might say. It's his empire, isn't it. The King's Road. And he got together with the girl, that Sandy. Because she was fixing the distribution, see what I mean.'

Yawning chasms of knowledge opened for Mischa. Yes, he saw what Nurse meant. It was obvious now. Little things that had happened. Things he had heard Sandy say. Passing Piccadilly Circus with her one night late, seeing the addicts drooping round the all-night chemist's. 'Silly kids. It's so easy to get when you know how.' Sandy was a pusher. She distributed the stuff, the snow, the horse, the heroin, the heavy roller. She had used his studio as a base for this operation. If anything had gone wrong he would have been suspect. Sandy's doing.

'Yes, Nurse. I see. I see what you mean.' He paused, wondering how to ask. He looked into Nurse's keen eyes. 'So where is Sandy now?'

Nurse wouldn't meet his gaze.

'Don't think about it, matey,' he mumbled. 'She's had her innings. Curtains. Finish. They took her away.'

Nurse got up, went into the galley again, and poured himself some tea, adding liquor from his hip flask. The mug steamed in the cold, stale air. He drank in noisy gulps.

Mischa lay quiet a long time. Painfully, sorrowfully, he remembered Sandy.

They'd been happy for a little while. Last Christmas, with her parents. And in the summer, here in the boat. Then came her 'friends', and wild parties in the saloon next-door. People known to the gossip columnists, many of them rich, talented, beautiful. The drugs they used. The way they laughed at him for his narrow, dedicated life. And the addicts gathering, squalid, pathetic. Syringes in the lavatory round the corner at the end of this bunk. Quarrels and arguments with Sandy. The end of their affair.

In the night, in midwinter, they had destroyed her beauty.

He must have been weeping, because when he lifted a stiff arm to look at his watch the figures were blurred by his tears. He blinked, and sent a few more rolling sideways over his cheeks. Nine-fifteen. Morning. The far porthole, overhung by the tarpaulin outside, was still dark, but the near one glowed pearly grey. There was light out there, and freedom. Distantly from the Embankment he could hear the noise of traffic. People were going to work, doing everyday things. In Nelson Square, less than a mile away, they were washing up breakfast, making beds, going shopping. He should be up, practising. But he lay idle, in a nightmare world.

Nurse had a gun. The portholes were sealed and very small. The door to the saloon was closed.

'It's locked, matey.' Nurse had been standing in the galley watching him, reading his thoughts. 'No good trying. Yours truly has the key. And that porthole don't open either.' He nodded towards the lavatory. 'And that other one, over there at mid-off, you can't see out of because we've covered the pitch for the winter. Sorry to disappoint, matey.'

'Yes, Nurse,' said Mischa.

He couldn't move much, anyway. He couldn't get up, fight Nurse, take the gun and run for it. Back to Nelson Square, Tim with the measles, Boney, John, Charlotte.

In his studio, all horror. Yamaguchi. And Sandy, somewhere else. They'd taken her away.

Nurse came back to his side and sat on the edge of the bunk, the smell of rum mingling with stale tobacco.

'Cheer up, matey. There's been an improvement in the weather conditions. You hear that dripping noise? It's thawing, that's what. We won't be bothered by too many footprints, see what I mean.'

'Yes, Nurse.'

'I'm doing my best for you, matey.'

'Yes, Nurse. Thank you. I was just thinking, you know. It was all a mistake. I wasn't going to come home till tomorrow. I mean today.'

'That's right, matey. We didn't expect the pleasure of your company.'

'It was because of the violin. The one in the crate that was for me,' explained Mischa.

'We left that one for you, matey. Don't worry. The boss wasn't interested. He checked in the case. No snow.'

'No snow. I was going to give it to someone.'

'Was it a kid?' asked Nurse.

'Yes.'

'There was a kid in the cupboard.' Mischa's heart missed a beat. 'The boss and the first eleven were busy on the crate –'

'Please.' Mischa grabbed Nurse's arm. His voice shook. 'Not Tim. Not Tim.'

'He's all right. Don't you worry. I seen that cupboard before, when I went to have my cuppa, bringing in the crate. So I hear something, I peek inside. There he is, in his pyjamas. Scarper, I whisper. Just a whisper. He went. Just like that. I leaned on the door, casual. We was almost finished. They'd got the consignment almost clear when you come along.'

Mischa's fingers relaxed.

'Then we make a hasty exit,' said Nurse. 'There was you to be got rid of, and the girl.' He sat silent for a while, took out a cigarette, lit it and blew smoke, shaking his head. 'I tell you, I'm through, matey. I don't want any more of it. Yours truly has had enough. So what about it?'

'What about what?'

'One good turn deserves another, matey. I mean, you've got friends, haven't you. Your ma and pa, maybe.'

'I don't see what you mean, Nurse.'

'Well, they'll want you back, won't they. They'll hand over a tidy sum. And I'll hand over Mr Lewis, the violinist. It's just a question of who we ask, matey. It's the ransom, isn't it.'

Mischa thought a long time.

'I don't have a pa and ma, Nurse,' he said. 'I had foster parents. They're dead. They never had much money.'

'Well, what about your management, or your friends in Chelsea? Come on, then. There must be somebody wants you back. What about the Musicians' Union, eh? I got to get away, matey, see what I mean. I got to get away and start a new life, and I'm all ready to go. I've been waiting a chance for years to change my address. I've got everything at the ready, buy a passport, away I go. All I need is the cash. I'm not asking a lot, just the cash to get away.' He was beginning to sound desperate. 'Otherwise it's curtains for you too, matey. See what I mean.'

'How much?' asked Mischa.

'Only a hundred thousand. Honestly, it's nothing. Only for my new life.'

'It's too much, Nurse. No one wants me that much. Say fifty thousand.'

'Make it seventy-five then, matey. Seventy-five thousand. Come on then. Who's it going to be?'

'I know someone,' said Mischa after a pause. 'Miss Margaret Robson. They call her Bobby.'

'She got the necessary?'

'She works on the *Chronicle*. Fleet Street.'

Nurse considered, then he smiled and his eyes twinkled. 'Clever. See what you mean, matey. She tells her boss and he gets the paper to offer a reward for information. Right?'

'Something like that.'

'Have to wait till tonight, matey. You see that, don't you. Cover of darkness. Ransom note got to be delivered by hand. It's tricky in daylight.'

'You could telephone her, Nurse. You see, if you work for a newspaper you have to be available day and night. She leaves a telephone number at the desk, wherever she is.'

'See what you mean, matey. How do I know it's her, though? Might get a fast bowler instead.'

'Fast bowler?'

'A copper, matey. Member of the Metropolitan Police Force. See what I mean.'

'Oh. Well, you'll know Bobby easily. She has a deep voice. She says Lord every time she speaks. Lord. Like that.'

'Might try her, matey.'

'It's an awful lot of money to ask, Nurse.'

'Can't do it for less, matey. Sorry.'

'I hope she can arrange something. She's a good friend of the editor. I hope it works out, Nurse.'

'So do I, matey. Bit of trouble otherwise. Now I wonder if there's any provisions I haven't found yet? You and I will be needing a spot of nourishment.'

'There used to be tins, in that locker above your head.'

'Didn't think of looking there, did I,' said Nurse, peering inside. 'See what I missed. Bit of all right. Baked beans. Spag. Tin peas. Tin apricots. Tin golden syrup. She had quite a stock of things, didn't she.'

Mischa lay staring at the ceiling above his bunk. He was warmer now and more comfortable. Thoughts fell into place. He was alive, and there was food and someone to look after him. And a gleam of hope. Perhaps the *Chronicle* out of its millions would pay seventy-five thousand pounds. Or perhaps someone would find him. Perhaps the police would get Nurse. And yet he liked him enough to hope that they wouldn't, if there was any other way.

He looked at his watch again. Had anyone missed him yet? It was half-past ten. His fingers stirred, longing for his violin. If he'd been at home he would have started practising by now. He thought of the studio and his music and last night's concert. And then, as if in a familiar nightmare, he imagined himself walking again down the square, past the last street lamp, shuffling through the snow, getting out his key and opening the door. Shortly after that, when they hit him, he must have dropped his violin and his overnight bag. He couldn't remember.

Stray thoughts returned and puzzled him.

'Nurse.'

'What's that, matey?'

'There were two other Japanese, you know. Yamaguchi's friends. What happened to them?'

'They scarpered, matey. Out to the boundary. We don't know where they went, and the boss was worried. Thought they might spread the glad tidings.'

Another pause, while Mischa thought and Nurse bustled round the stove.

'Nurse, I'm sorry I keep bothering you. There were all those people in the studio last night, you and the boss and the others. How did you get in? Did you break a window?'

Nurse, holding a can of beans in one hand and a tin-opener in the other, looked him squarely in the eye.

'She had a key, matey. That girl, that Sandy.'

Of course. Long ago, when they were happy, he'd given her a key. He'd forgotten.

That Sandy.

She'd betrayed him.

3

At ten in the morning Geraldine rang our doorbell and made her routine inquiry about the bike. I told her about Tim. He had kept Madeleine awake for quite a while, and she was only just getting up.

'Pneumonia is bad, definitely,' said Geraldine. 'Poor kid. Never you mind about her bike then. Tell her nobody can move these vehicles anyway, they still covered with snow down this end.'

In fact it had stopped snowing and there had been a dramatic change in the weather. I fetched a broom, cleared the front steps, and went out to survey the scene from the pavement. The King's Road end of the square was bathed in pale sunlight. It was so much warmer now that it seemed almost hot, like spring. The snow was thawing and dripping away, and mist rose from it as if it were simmering with heat. Melting slabs slithered gently from car roofs and collapsed in the gutter. But we were still in the shade, down at twenty-three, and winter lingered. Round the corner, by the studio door and all down Lot's Passage, the snow was still thick and white.

'I got that bad Honda, see,' said Geraldine, pointing. 'He left it there all night, and I booked him this time. My, he's getting very sloppy. He left his door open.'

The Honda certainly had a neglected look. It was crookedly parked, one window was half rolled down and the nearside door was open and hanging over the pavement. Geraldine slammed it shut and stuck her ticket in the windscreen-wiper.

'That you, Geraldine?' said Boney. 'Come on, you need a cup of coffee, don't you. Won't take five minutes.'

'Just the once, then.' Geraldine stepped in and wiped her boots carefully on the mat. 'I won't say No as I been up since six this morning.'

We gathered in the kitchen. John was up and dressed for a change, and he and Madeleine were having a late breakfast. She said Tim was asleep now and it looked as if the antibiotic had started working. The doctor would be round soon.

'Poor man,' she said. 'He probably gets woken most nights all through the winter. Gosh, who would be a doctor.'

'I would, Madeleine,' said Boney. 'If I had your brains. Meanwhile I best get on with my cleaning.'

She opened the broom cupboard and squeezed inside, muttering that she'd do the studio first as Mischa was away.

'What you going to be, John?' asked Geraldine, 'when you get big?'

'Racing driver,' said John. 'Or zoologist if I get any A-Levels.'

'You could easily if you worked harder,' I reminded him.

'I haven't got your carbonated brains,' said John. 'Even if I do work hard nothing much seems to happen –'

And then we heard Boney's scream.

A tearing terrible noise, through in the studio. So terrible that all of us knew immediately that this was no joke, no ordinary event. Not a mouse scuttling across the shiny floor, nor a leaky roof, nor an untidy pile of music left lying on the piano, nor dirty dishes in Mischa's sink.

Fear.

I was nearest. I stumbled through the cupboard. The others were behind me, Madeleine and Geraldine and John. I had to go on, and see.

Boney leaned against the wall, grey-faced, panting. She pointed. The studio was a mess, wood-shavings, paper, cardboard boxes torn in pieces, the crate standing open and empty.

'What?' I grasped Boney's arm. 'What is it? Where?'

She clutched her heart. 'Police! Don't look. It's over there. Get the police!'

I had to look. We all had to look. We walked slowly forward into the studio, round the crate.

Mr Yamaguchi lay dead on the floor. His head was curiously twisted. There was blood on his chest. All around lay rubbish.

'It's vile,' breathed John. 'Vile, horrible. Ugh!'

Geraldine put her hands on her hips and slowly shook her head.

'It's that Honda,' she said. 'My oh my, that bad Honda!'

Boney swayed, almost fainting. Madeleine gave the orders and we obeyed. All out. Don't touch anything. Back through the cupboard. A terrible effort, supporting the sagging, heavy Boney, knocking brooms and brushes to the floor. Into the kitchen, safe.

We got Boney into a chair and Madeleine shoved her head down. It was difficult. She wasn't the right shape. But it worked and the colour came back to her cheeks.

'I'll be all right in half a minute,' she apologized, fanning herself with the *Daily Express*. 'Oh dear. Oh dear. I'm so glad it was me and not Mischa. Oh dear.'

'Keep sitting down for a while,' ordered Madeleine, pouring her a glass of water at the sink.

'That's right,' said Geraldine. 'You all stay here. I better telephone them at the station, definitely.'

News travels fast in Nelson Square. By the time the black police Jaguar arrived, the Admiral and Skipper were on the doorstep, and so was Fred. We brought them inside. They were friends and we needed them.

'Bad show,' said the Admiral. 'You've certainly had a nasty time of it.'

'From the beginning,' said Geraldine, 'I had the feeling he was bad, that Honda. But did I ever think of robbery and murder? My oh my. The other Honda men robbed the crate and then they murdered him. They left their vehicle with the nearside door open –'

She shuddered and wrung her hands.

'Never you mind, sweetheart,' said Fred, taking advantage of the crisis to put his arm round her shoulders and give her a good squeeze. 'You got a shock, didn't you. I seen some sights in my time, I know how you feel. That time I found the poor lady lying dead in her kitchen. It was a stroke she had, but we had to call the police just the same.'

Boney had recovered and felt rather ashamed.

'I don't know what came over me. I'm a silly old fool, aren't I. Put on the kettle for me, Charlotte. There's a dear. I'll make a big pot of tea, enough for all of us. And them.'

She nodded in the direction of the studio. A uniformed inspector, a plain-clothes man, two police constables and a sergeant were in there, with Madeleine. Boney had offered to open Mischa's front door for them with the spare key, but was turned down. They had all filed through our kitchen and into the studio through the broom cupboard. John was fascinated. He followed as far as he could in the hopes of overhearing something through the door, but Boney called him away.

'Behave yourself, John. They'll call us if they need us. Poor Mischa. That's going to be a nasty surprise for him. Can't think what they were doing in there, breaking open that crate.'

'Stealing violins,' said John. 'It's obvious. They were probably valuable ones after all. People make a fortune out of stolen antiques.'

'There's the doorbell again,' said Boney. 'You can make yourself valuable by going and seeing who it is.'

John rushed off, hoping for more excitement, but it was only the doctor.

'What on earth's going on?' he asked. 'Nothing to do with you, I hope.'

'Not guilty,' said John. 'But it looks like murder.'

Boney took the doctor upstairs, explaining volubly. He

thought Tim was doing all right. It would be another twenty-four hours before the virus succumbed, three or four days until he was back to something like normal. Meanwhile what about hospital? He could arrange it. Would it help?

'I wouldn't dream of it, Doctor,' protested Boney. 'I know the circumstances are unusual, goings-on next door and everything. But I wouldn't feel right with someone else looking after our Tim. There's two of us, me and Madeleine. And Charlotte. And he's warm and comfortable. We'll manage him. We won't say anything about what's happening. His curtains are closed because of the light, so he won't notice.'

The doctor left, followed by the Admiral, Skipper, Geraldine and Fred. The house seemed suddenly empty. I wandered to and fro, feeling unsettled and miserable. Something was badly wrong and I couldn't think what it was. I sat for a while in the front window, looking out from behind the curtains. Passers-by in the King's Road had sensed that something had happened. They stopped at the corner and talked to Mick, who was giving a running commentary on developments, and then they came on down the square and stood staring outside the studio. Another sergeant arrived and was planting police notices at each end of Lot's Passage so that no one could go through. Two constables were prodding the remaining snow with spades and digging holes in it. Then they swept the slush off Mischa's step, very carefully, into a dustpan, and took it away. A police van brought lights and other equipment. 'Cameras,' said John. People stayed a little while, watching the police coming and going, then moved on. I looked hopefully at everybody who turned into the square.

No Mischa.

Madeleine reappeared from next door. She'd been there

over an hour. The Inspector's compliments and would Mrs Bowen kindly step into the studio, using the broom cupboard and not the front entrance, please?

Boney patted her hair, took off her apron and pulled down her sweater.

'How do I look?' she asked. 'I used to have a boyfriend in the Force, years ago. Before I met the old man. I quite fancy a policeman.'

'You look smashing,' said Madeleine. 'He's awfully nice. .We'll lay the lunch for you. Come on, Charlotte.'

Almost lunch-time, and still no Mischa. He liked to get home as soon as possible. There was the precious routine of practising.

'Come on, Charlotte.'

'Sorry.' I followed Madeleine into the kitchen. 'I just wish Mischa would come back and get it over.'

We laid the table and a tray for Tim. I offered to take it up and as I reached the landing my hands started trembling and I had to put it down on the top step. Of course, I remembered now. In the middle of the night.

I saw Mischa coming. I went down to the cupboard. I was frightened.

Had he really said that? Had he really seen Mischa coming back? And if so, what had happened and where was Mischa now?

Sitting on the landing my thoughts went wild. I tried to think straight. Not our Mischa. He couldn't do anything like that, anything violent or harmful, with those hands. He was an artist, a genius. It couldn't possibly happen. But then sometimes a genius could be just on the edge of sanity, so brilliant as to be almost unbalanced.

Mad.

He couldn't be. Not our Mischa.

Then I remembered *Assignment*, and the other films he'd enjoyed. Stupid highly-coloured stuff, robberies, shooting, violence, spectacular car chases.

Please, please, not our Mischa.

I took a big breath and picked up the tray and took it into Tim's room. He lay quietly in semi-darkness, awake, snuggling under the blankets.

'I'm a bit cold,' he said cheerfully. 'I been sleeping and I woke up all sweaty. Look.'

He was damp all over, pyjamas, hair, sheets and pillows all wet. His forehead was cool and damp. I called Madeleine and we wrapped him in a blanket and re-made his bed and found him some more pyjamas.

'Clever Tim,' said Madeleine. 'You're sweating it out. It's the best way.'

'I think I'll have another sweat after lunch,' said Tim. 'It makes you feel better. Except you get bad dreams with it.'

His soup had got cold and I had to take it downstairs to warm it up again. We sat with him while he ate a little. He still wasn't very hungry but he seemed better. He lay down again and we tucked him up.

'Has Mischa come back yet?' he said suddenly.

'No,' said Madeleine. 'We'll tell you as soon as he does.'

'I dreamed about him in the night. And my violin. It was frightening.'

'Yes,' said Madeleine. 'Dreams are funny sometimes, aren't they. There. Now you're all warm and tidy again. Can we get him a bell of some sort, Charlotte? Then he can ring if he needs us. If he's going to sweat it's the best possible thing, but he'll need to be changed every time.'

We went downstairs. Of course it was only a dream. He hadn't really seen Mischa. And Mischa would be back soon, surely. Any minute. He'd be coming round the corner in his concert overcoat.

'You look a bit white in the face,' Madeleine was saying. 'Do you like sherry? Why don't we have some from the bottle I bought yesterday? It's rather civilized before lunch.'

The police sent for John. He was thrilled. He couldn't wait to get into the studio and see what was going on. They wanted his fingerprints because he had helped bring in the crate. What if they sent for me next? What if they asked me what I knew? What if I broke down, when they bullied me, and told them everything and Mischa was found guilty?

A murderer.

If only he would come back. If only I could see him and be sure.

'C.I.D. of course,' said Boney at lunch. 'He was so polite. I told him everything and he said I'd been most helpful. I invited him to come and have a bite with us, but he said he'd go back to the station. They'll be busy in the studio for a while. Mischa will have to come and sleep in the study, just for tonight.'

'They've got little saucers of stuff to analyze,' said John. 'Dust and bits of paper and fluff. They've got all the things out of Mischa's fridge and his toothpaste and soap, everything. It's spread out on the floor, in rows.'

'Mischa's awfully late,' said Boney. 'He was back for lunch that other time he went to Birmingham, for the rehearsal, wasn't he. Can you manage another potato, John?'

'Yes, please. They said I was very helpful. I described the van and the driver. And I saw the body. It was covered with a blanket –'

I got up and pushed in my chair

'Sorry, I don't feel hungry, Boney.'

I went upstairs and lay on my bed. I couldn't do anything.

I couldn't play records without thinking of Mischa, even Blues records. I couldn't read. I didn't want to talk to anybody. I kept thinking about him and what might have happened in the night. How Tim might have woken up and looked out into the square. Snow falling. Mischa coming home, secretly.

My bedroom, on the top floor at the back of the house, looked the other way, over people's roofs and chimney-pots. And John's room was directly below mine. Tim and the parents faced the square. And so did the spare room, on the top floor opposite mine. So if Madeleine had looked out she would have seen Mischa too.

Horrible thoughts went round in my head. After a while I decided that lying down made it worse, so I got up and went downstairs again and had some coffee and a sandwich. Everyone was very nice to me.

'Sorry,' said John. 'I didn't know you were such a sensitive old charlady.'

A police van took Mr Yamaguchi away. A stretcher, blanket-covered. A police truck towed away his Honda. The Inspector returned from lunch, stayed ten minutes and left. A sergeant waited in the studio, a constable on the step, a police car outside in the square. Sightseers dispersed, to get on with their Christmas shopping. There was nothing much to see. The afternoon wore on and it began to get dark.

Still no Mischa.

I went out to do some shopping for Boney. On the way back I stopped to talk to Mick. His barrow was lit with a string of Christmas tree lights. His fruit and vegetables glowed pink, green and blue.

'Cor. They been busy at your place, haven't they. Calling in the Yard.'

'The Yard?'

'Yes, I seen them going in. You remember that case over

Wandsworth, that drugs case and the teenage kids? I know his face from then. Inspector from Scotland Yard. Inspector Gregson.'

'What for, Mick?'

'There's a body then. That's one thing. Your Division deals with that, luv. But something else and they call in the Yard.'

'What else?'

'Things like drugs, luv. Cor. You need a specialist, don't you. Someone who knows all about it. How's Tim then?'

'He's a bit better. He loves the aeroplane. He had it on his pillow all yesterday.'

'What about your Mischa then? They'll want to see him, won't they.'

'Yes, Mick.'

'Where is he, luv, excuse me asking?'

'Well, you see the trains have been held up by snow.'

'That's it then. Well, goodnight. I'm packing it in.'

He put out his lights, detached them from the battery and rolled up the flex.

I walked miserably down the square. A few lumps of snow gleamed in cold corners. Otherwise the thaw had melted most of it away. As I got nearer the bottom I went a little faster. Perhaps Mischa was back. If he'd taken a taxi he might have come home without Mick seeing him. He might be inside having tea. Our Mischa.

There were two police cars there now. A different constable stood in Mischa's doorway. I smiled at him and let myself into twenty-three.

I dumped the parcels and started taking off my coat. Boney came hurrying out of the kitchen with Madeleine and John after her.

'Oh Charlotte.' Boney, the big strong reliable Boney, had been crying. She was wiping her eyes. 'Oh dear. There's another inspector there now, he's from Scotland Yard. They found traces of drugs, I don't know. Something dreadful. It couldn't be our Mischa. He never touched anything like that.'

I couldn't speak.

'He doesn't even smoke,' said John. 'He wouldn't touch drugs. The police put them there. I've read about it, often.'

'Oh dear. I told them everything I could, I know it's nothing to do with our Mischa. But he hasn't come home yet – and – and –' Boney burst into tears, buried her face in a handkerchief and went away.

'What happened?' I asked Madeleine. 'Please tell me.'

'They don't know where he is, Charlotte. They got in touch with Birmingham. Apparently he didn't spend the night there at all. He got a lift back to London with Mirmanov, in a hired car. They're getting in touch with the driver. And Interpol will talk to Mirmanov, in Zurich. They were the last people to see him.'

We sat down together on the window-seat. John stood in front of us, kicking the edge of the carpet.

'It's vile,' he said.

'They know he got home.' Madeleine's voice was calm and sensible. But I couldn't look at her. 'His violin case and his bag were in the hall. And his key was lying underneath them. But they didn't find any of his fingerprints on the crate. They found John's, because he helped bring it in. And Boney's. None of Mischa's.'

'It was fun being fingerprinted,' said John. 'But everything else is so vile.'

I kept my eyes down, watching John's restless feet, trying to remember that moment when I'd found Tim on the landing in the night. What had he actually said? I couldn't think clearly.

'Then this afternoon,' went on Madeleine, 'they found something else in Lot's Passage. You see, it snowed again during the night and there might have been footprints which were covered up. And this got covered too. I'm so sorry. I had to tell you.'

'What do you mean? What got covered?'

'His hat. It's a fur hat and Boney identified it. There was blood inside it. Gosh, I'm sorry Charlotte.'

John stopped kicking the carpet and came and sat next to me. He seemed much smaller, more like the horrible little eight-year-old he used to be. I put my arm around him.

We sat there for quite a while. The sitting-room was dark and only the street lamps outside lit us up. Boney came back, sniffing, and sat in an armchair. We were very quiet. There seemed to be nothing for us to do. Next-door in the studio Scotland Yard were doing it for us. We seemed to have reached the bottom of some horrible pit of despair, where everything was strange and terrifying. We couldn't easily get out of it.

Then gradually one by one we revived. We started hoping again. We began to talk, bolstering ourselves up, telling each other that it would all come right in the end. We'd hear something soon, very soon, news of Mischa. It would be good news. It would be all right.

'I rang Bobby,' said Boney. 'She's coming round. Oh dear. She said she'd stay the night and sleep in the study. She's talking to the editor, trying to keep it out of the papers. Oh dear. I can't believe this is happening.'

'I'm sure he's all right,' said John. 'He's very strong and he does yoga and he's in training. Musicians have to be athletes.'

'I can't believe it,' said Boney again.

We watched the news on television. Luckily the freak snowstorm seemed to be more important than anything else that day. There had been a spectacular fire in a warehouse in the East End, which took up a bit of coverage too. The body found in the studio of Mischa Lewis, the violinist, was just mentioned. And that he had been away in Birmingham at the time. There was a picture of his front door, nothing else. Police were making enquiries.

Bobby came in time for supper. She was her steady cheerful self. She was a rock. We felt better with her there.

'It's lucky your parents aren't expecting daily reports,' she said at supper. 'Lord, they'd have a fit.'

'When's the first link?' said John.

'Boxing Day.'

'We'll have found him by then.'

'I wish you wouldn't keep on about it,' I protested.

'But I know we will. We'll ask everyone what they know. We'll make our own enquiries. The police are awful fools.'

'I shouldn't say that, John,' said Boney. 'They've been very civil and clever so far, if you ask me. Come on, let's get the table cleared. Then we'll watch *Comedy Crew*. It'll keep our minds off it. We'll skip the news.'

During the evening the telephone hardly stopped ringing. Most of the calls were from Mischa's friends. They'd rung the studio and been fobbed off by the police. They were puzzled and upset. Worst of all was John Mackintosh, the pianist. He'd seen the evening papers. What was going on, he wanted to know, and how could he get in touch? Madeleine answered. She told him Mischa was spending the night with friends. We didn't know their address or telephone number. Mac wouldn't believe her.

'Gosh, was he angry,' she said, coming back from the telephone pink in the face. 'Swearing in fluent Scotch. What else could I say?'

We agreed she'd done the right thing. We put out the same story to all enquirers. They seemed to hate us. It was unfair.

Mercifully the time passed. John was tired, yawning. He got up reluctantly to go to bed.

'I'm not scared or anything,' he explained. 'It's just that I want to be awake if anything happens. If he comes back.'

'Stop it!' I snapped, and was immediately sorry and had to apologise. 'Come on, I'm going to bed too. Leave your door open and I'll leave mine.'

The shortest day was coming to an end. Gradually we dispersed, Boney to the basement with a sleeping pill prescribed by the doctor for the occasion. 'Never used them before in my life,' she said. Bobby to the study. The rest of us upstairs. Tim was sleeping peacefully after several more heavy sweats. Madeleine and I started up to the top floor together.

'He's doing very well,' she said. 'He'll be a bit feeble and bad-tempered afterwards, but we can bear that, can't we.'

Inside I knew I could bear anything if only I could be sure that Mischa was all right. I told her. And then I found I was telling her all sorts of other things as well. It came pouring out, everything right from the beginning, about that first evening at the end of the summer holidays when we'd seen Chairman Miaow, about Mrs Kawate and the fake Guarnerius, and Graham and Sandy Lovelace, about Mr Yamaguchi and his friends and the Honda which hung about our part of the King's Road. And Tim's dream.

'If only you'd told me,' she murmured, listening wide-eyed. 'If only you'd told me sooner.'

'I can't explain,' I rambled on. 'It was all part of life. It was little things happening every day. Things people said, people like Mick and Fred. And I was working all the time for that rotten exam and I didn't really pay enough attention. I mean, perhaps something was there right under my nose. Something awful, for Mischa. Perhaps he had a secret life we didn't know about. He got muddled up with these people—'

'No.' Madeleine shook her red head firmly.

'How can you tell? You don't even know him.'

'He is an artist, Charlotte. A musician. He's not the sort of person to care about other things, outside. Music is his life.'

She was quite right. If ever this was true it was true of Mischa. He only seemed like an ordinary person. He was alive. He ate and drank. He liked people and jokes and an occasional party. He was interested in books and old furniture. But the thing that really mattered was music, his music, his own personal part of the world which he filled with the noise of his violin. Sonatas were his life, concertos, partitas, chaconnes, all the wonderful things written for his instrument. Rippling cadenzas, slow exquisitely balanced scales, beautifully articulated trills, those were the things that mattered. The slippery feel of the E string, the smoother A, the rough G and D, the sound that came singing into the air as his bow passed over them.

Music was his life.

'I can't bear it if he's dead, Madeleine.'

'Gosh, don't be silly. Of course he's not dead.'

'I wish I could do something,' I said. 'I wish I could help. We're all sitting here being brave and we're not any nearer finding him. If he's alive.'

'There's one thing you can do which would help, but I don't think you're going to like it.' She shrugged her skinny shoulders and looked at me sideways. 'Something that would really help.'

'What? I'll do anything, you know I will.'

'Come downstairs and speak to the Inspector. Tell him what you told me. Come on. He's still in the studio, I know he is. His car's still outside.'

I argued. I tried to get out of it. She bullied me until I said yes, and in case I weakened she came with me. We went quietly downstairs into the kitchen, tiptoeing past the study where Bobby was tucked up on the couch. We went bravely into the broom cupboard, huddling together in the darkness, smelling dust and floor polish. A sliver of light from the studio shone underneath the door. We knocked. We waited quite a while, hearing voices droning.

'Knock again,' I hissed. 'Before I change my mind.'

'Be brave,' whispered Madeleine. 'You'll be glad afterwards. He's called Gregson. Detective Inspector Gregson.'

The door opened rather suddenly. We felt like silly schoolgirls.

'Thought I heard something,' said the very young constable who seemed to be the Inspector's personal assistant. He was pink-faced and awkward and didn't quite know what to do about us. 'We're busy in here, you know.'

'My friend wants to tell the Inspector something,' said Madeleine. 'It's something very important. We know it's late but –'

'Half a minute.'

He closed the door while he consulted and then he let us in. We blinked in the light. The studio looked strange. Mischa's table had been pulled out into the middle of the room and Inspector Gregson was sitting there with a pile of papers in front of him. Beside him was the standard lamp which belonged over by the piano. The piano had been pushed against the wall. Mischa's music was laid on the floor in piles with little tickets sticking out here and there. The crate was spread out in pieces and a sergeant and a plain-clothes man were kneeling down making notes. The wood-shavings and paper were in another corner, arranged in heaps like sandcastles. The constable had Mischa's kitchen table to work on, with a typewriter and Mischa's bedside light. I felt miserable, looking at all his possessions rearranged.

'Please come in.' The Inspector was very polite, not what I'd expected, brisk, good-looking, bright blue eyes, a single-breasted pinstripe suite, spotted tie. We shook hands. 'Things are a bit untidy, but we'll have it all sorted out by the morning. Routine, most of it. Let's have a couple of chairs, Grainger. We met this afternoon, briefly,' he said, smiling at Madeleine. 'This must be Miss Charlotte Beresford, right?'

'She's Firth,' explained Madeleine. 'You see her mother is Charlotta Firth and Charlotte was her child by her first marriage and she married someone else afterwards but she always kept the name Firth and that's her professional name too. She's always called Charlotta Firth. Then she married Alan Beresford and John was Alan's son by his first marriage and Tim is –'

'Fine, fine,' said the Inspector. 'Got the gist of that, Grainger?'

'Thank you sir.' The young constable was taking notes on a shorthand pad.

'Well, I beg your pardon, Miss Firth,' said the Inspector. 'I should have known better. Mrs Bowen mentioned that you are hoping to get to Cambridge. I'm a red-brick man myself, Leeds –'

This didn't seem to be what I'd come to tell him about, but I found myself explaining why Cambridge was my first choice, and then I mentioned Graham who was at Leeds, and the Inspector mentioned Mischa's concert in Birmingham and we were off. I lowered my voice and he said several times, 'Sorry, I didn't quite catch.'

'I think she doesn't want everyone to know about it,' explained Madeleine kindly. 'It's rather personal.'

'Don't worry,' said Inspector Gregson. 'The sarge and company are so wrapped up in their work they wouldn't be listening anyway, and Grainger here is rather deaf. Isn't that so, Grainger?' he added in a loud voice. 'Grainger! I said are you deaf?'

'Sorry sir,' said the constable, looking up suddenly. 'Did you say something?'

'What did I tell you,' said the Inspector. 'You speak in your ordinary voice, Miss Firth. He's a nice enough chap, just a bit dreamy.'

Grainger went on writing all the same.

I began at the beginning. The Inspector said very little. He doodled. He drew little flowers and put legs on them, and eyes with very long lashes which grew leaves. They spread towards me all over his pad. They were very soothing and it made it much easier to talk. I told him about Chairman Miaow, first, and the Rs pronounced as Ls, the Bentley waiting at the bottom of Lot's Passage. Then about the letter from Japan and Mrs Kawate and the fake Guarnerius, which Mischa said Tim could have.

'Excuse me, sorry to interrupt.' The Inspector held up a finger for me to stop. 'Grainger!'

'Sorry, sir?' The constable, all surprised innocence, put down his pencil.

'Letter from er –' He fumbled among his papers. 'Here we are. Mitsura Export-Import. Number fifty-three in that pile over there. If you can't find it ask Sarge.'

The letter was produced. The white silky paper. The neat typing. No signature.

'Yes,' I said. 'That's it.' I remembered, too vividly, Mischa in the kitchen, the laughing and fooling about and Tim hanging on to him, wanting him to stay for lunch. I dried up for a while.

'You see,' said Madeleine, to fill the gap, 'Charlotte has known Mischa for an awful long time and what's happened is terrible. She can't help thinking that you might think he did it, or that he might have known about these people and the drugs, or whatever it is. But she knows that he's not that sort of person, he never was and he never could be and music is his whole life –'

Grainger had to write very fast. Madeleine was quite a talker.

'Here, Grainger. Put this back where it belongs.' The Inspector handed him the letter, watched his retreating back and lent over the table towards us. 'Off the record, ladies,' he said quietly, 'I want you to know that I am already convinced that what you say is correct. I don't know Mischa Lewis personally, though I have heard him play on several occasions, but I do know two things for sure. One, that he didn't do it, as you put it, by which I presume that you mean he didn't kill Mr Yamaguchi. Right? And two, that he didn't know what was going on here in the early hours of this morning. Let's go on.'

Grainger came back and sat down. Inspector Gregson resumed his doodling. A little Christmas tree grew under his ballpoint, with baubles on it which sprouted rays of light which branched out into veins which made other trees.

'Next Mr Yamaguchi came to the door,' prompted Madeleine.

I went on. Mr Yamaguchi. Sandy Lovelace. How she'd broken with Mischa. How we'd met her in the King's Road, Tim and I. How Tim had told her that we were going away for Christmas.

The Inspector's ballpoint hesitated in the middle of a pretty scroll with two little legs on it.

'What was she wearing?' he asked.

'Oh, a super expensive fur coat, golden-coloured, like her hair, and brown boots. And she had a golden Mini.'

'Go on.' The doodling recommenced. He added feet on to the two little legs, and shoes with bows on them.

Then I told him what Mick had said. About Mr Lee, the big boss, who owned the Chinese restaurant and the Judo

Jim and the Karate Klub, and how I felt sure he was the same large slit-eyed man who had come to our door, way back in September.

'So there's a man called Mick who has a barrow on the corner of the King's Road. Surname? Never mind. Right. And Fred the milkman. We'll get someone from the Division to see him at the depot early tomorrow. Wonderful witnesses, milkmen. And Geraldine. Yes, she's made a statement already. Miss Geraldine Tracy Fletcher, traffic warden. She's a bright girl, very observant. Go on.'

'When I was working for my exam I got very tired and cross, and Alan, that's my stepfather, took me for a walk one night and said I mustn't work so hard. And we went along the Embankment and I saw the same man again, Mr Lee. At least I think he's the same man as the one John and I saw, that first time. And there was a girl with him and she looked a bit like Sandy. It was in November. No, it was before my birthday. So it was October, about the second week.'

As if this were only of passing interest the Inspector asked where I had seen them, exactly, and where Alan and I were, and how dark it was. He kept drawing. He hardly looked at me.

'Is Miss Lovelace a friend of yours?'

'No. I don't like her. She was horrible to Mischa and I think he was hurt.'

'Miss Firth, you're completely frank, which is a great help. May I ask you another question, a personal one?'

I nodded.

'Was Mischa Lewis your boyfriend at any stage? I mean, did you feel jealous of his attachment to Miss Lovelace?'

'No. No. Of course not.' I was appalled.

'You don't understand,' said Madeleine. 'Mischa is like a big brother, he's been here since she was – how old, Charlotte? Eleven or twelve. He's part of the family. She's got a boyfriend, the one who's at Leeds University, but things went a bit wrong –'

'Oh never mind,' I said. 'We don't have to bring that up.'

'Well, I beg your pardon,' said the Inspector. 'I really went a bit far, didn't I. We policemen are coarse-minded brutes. Forgive me. Now, what next?'

Tim's dream. I sat silent a long while, trying to remember what he'd said. The actual words.

'Last night. No, early this morning. You see, Tim's room is at the front. Next to the parents. I heard him crying and I went down. I thought he'd had a bad dream. He was on the landing. He said –' I put my head in my hands. What had he said? 'He said he'd gone downstairs to see his violin. The one I told you about. He said he'd seen Mischa coming and then he couldn't sleep and he went down to the cupboard. He was frightened. He was shaking, but he had pneumonia. Madeleine telephoned the doctor. That's all.'

'Tim might have been murdered,' whispered Madeleine.

'Any idea what time it was?' asked the Inspector.

'It was five to four.'

'By your watch?'

'No, because I take it off to sleep and it was by my bed but I didn't look at it when I got up to go to Tim. I was downstairs, boiling the kettle for a hot-water bottle, later on, and I saw the kitchen clock.'

The Inspector asked for the doctor's name.

'Check time,' he murmured in a low voice. Grainger, surprisingly, heard him perfectly and said 'Yes sir.'

'Yes, it was about four,' said Madeleine helpfully.

The Inspector, expressionless, laid down his ballpoint, got up and went over to speak to the sergeant and the plain-clothes man. They said goodnight and left. Grainger leaned forward on Mischa's kitchen table and closed his eyes.

It was midnight. The end of the horrible nightmare day.

I was just asking Madeleine if we should get up and go, as they didn't seem to want us any more, when the Inspector came back. He had a glass saucer in his hand, covered with transparent plastic.

'I'm sorry to delay you, Miss Firth. When do you think Miss Lovelace was last here, in this studio?'

'She hasn't been for ages. Not since the summer.'

He looked me in the eye.

'We think she was here last night. Here' – he held out the saucer – 'here we have something which might be fur from the coat you described.'

We looked. A few long stiff browny-gold hairs lay there, and a tuft of blond fluff. I was frightened. He was watching me so closely.

'You said, Miss Firth, that when you met Miss Lovelace shopping she had a car and she got into it and drove away. A gold-finish Mini, with dark windows.'

'Yes.'

'It's called Florentine Gold, Inspector,' said Grainger, lifting his weary head.

'Right. Florentine Gold.' He turned back to me and the blue eyes twinkled cold and bright. 'Now, we've spoken to the driver who brought Mr Mirmanov and Mr Lewis to London. He says he dropped Mr Lewis at the entrance to Nelson Square, in the King's Road, at three-twenty. He turned left at Martineau Street and left again on to the Embankment. He proceeded towards Chelsea Bridge. He says he believes he saw two vehicles parked at the bottom of Lot's Passage. One was a yellow Bedford van like the one which your brother John described to me this morning in such glowing detail –'

'My stepbrother, not my brother.'

'– the other was a Mini in whatever Grainger said. Florentine Gold. During the course of routine inquiries we found a similar vehicle in the multi-storey car park at London Airport. There were bloodstains in the back seat.' He paused. 'I don't know if you heard the news late this evening. No. Well, the body of a blonde girl, dressed in a fur coat and brown boots, was found on a piece of waste-ground near Hounslow just before dark. She had been dead approximately twelve hours. The body is in the mortuary awaiting positive identification. Her handbag is missing, but from a quick check of the numerous photographs available we are pretty sure that she was Miss Sandy Lovelace.'

I heard Madeleine gasp, but I wasn't frightened any more. I looked fearlessly at Inspector Gregson, right into his deceptive blue eyes. All that friendliness and charm, and what a stupid clumsy policeman he turned out to be.

'All this is nothing to do with Mischa,' I said crushingly. 'He is a violinist and his hands are so precious to him that he won't learn to drive a car. My stepfather offered to teach him but he wouldn't hear of it. He doesn't even like to sit in the front of one. He sits in the back whenever he can. He won't ride a bicycle. His hands are for his music, for playing the violin, which is his life. And' – I felt a fine anger rising in me – 'if Sandy Lovelace got mixed up with drugs and Mr Lee and Yamaguchi that's her own affair and nothing to do with Mischa either. She was an awful person. Mischa didn't like her friends. Some of them were on drugs and that's one of the reasons they quarrelled. He told me. Also she said she couldn't wait for him to get famous. That was cruel. I told you I didn't like her, and I'm sorry she's dead, but I still feel the same.'

I took a breath, glowing with rage. To my surprise the Inspector clapped his hands and beamed all over.

'Bravo!' he cried. 'Miss Firth, I apologize for being so unkind to you. You're a bright girl and I'll be very surprised if you don't get into the university of your choice. Can we shake hands?'

We shook hands.

'We'd better go,' said Madeleine. 'It's awfully late.'

'Yes,' said the Inspector. 'One last thing. Mrs Bowen said your brother Tim – sorry, your half-brother, Miss Firth – keeps asking for his violin. It's here. Would you like to see it?'

We followed him across the studio. He lifted a brown cloth labelled 'Violin – Number Seven'. Underneath was an old-fashioned wooden violin case, with one brass catch missing. He picked it up and laid it on top of the piano.

'This is the violin which a Japanese pianist, Mrs Rose Kawate, left to Mr Mischa Lewis in her will. Quite innocently she left him a load of trouble, too. There were six other violins in the crate which was brought to the studio through the agency of Mr Yamaguchi, as he called himself. This was not his real name. He was a shady character known to Interpol. And there is no such firm as Mitsura Export-Import. It was invented for the occasion. What we are looking for now is the crooked exporter who master-minded the operation, who'd been on the look-out for bequests or shipments of a personal sort going to Europe, which could be used as cover. Enquiries are going ahead. Chelsea Division found traces of heroin in the crate. We believe the other violins, which were probably those mass-produced instruments which the Japanese make so well, were filled with heroin in small packets. Yamaguchi was going to take delivery direct from Mr Lewis, all open and above board. Someone else got in first, when the place was empty.'

'Can I ask something?' said Madeleine. 'What were Mr Yamaguchi's injuries?'

'He died of a broken neck. The stab wound was added afterwards.'

'That's interesting, gosh,' said Madeleine. 'A man came into our hospital the other day. They said he'd been in a knife fight, and then the surgeon found –'

They chatted away. I yawned. My eyes were heavy. It was so late and I was terribly sleepy.

'No sign of the other violins,' the Inspector was saying. 'But we'll find them. In my opinion the intruders were surprised in the act, and had to disband hastily. They'll be disorganized. They'll slip up. With any luck we'll recover something like twenty-five pounds weight of heroin.'

'That's worth a lot of money, isn't it?' Madeleine was wide-awake.

The Inspector nodded.

'Worth a fortune. We're working out how much they could get in. The Japanese are expert packers, so there would have been no wasted space. We're going to have a mock-up, this crate here filled with lightweight violins, packets of powder of the same specific gravity as heroin. We've got the declared weight of the whole thing for shipping –'

I yawned again. How they talked.

'We had Mr Lewis's fingerprints, of course. His own violin, and his possessions here. But there were none of them on this case or on the instrument. So we presume he didn't handle it, unless he wore gloves. Which is unlikely. He would certainly have taken them off, particularly if they were wet with snow, to pick up this violin.'

He opened the case. The inside was lined with moth-eaten blue felt. Two bows with trailing hairs were pinned into the lid under ivory latches. The violin lay under an embroidered silk cover, looking very sad, like a small brown corpse. The E and D strings were broken. It looked as if it hadn't been played for years. Old and dim and dead.

'We had to dust it for fingerprints,' said the Inspector.

'Sorry about that. The varnish looks a bit cloudy. But don't worry, it'll wipe off. Linseed oil is the right thing. Incidentally,' he added, showing off more knowledge, 'I had a look at the label. A Guarnerius. Del Gesù 1740.'

'Labels are nothing to go by,' I said wearily. 'They used to make these fakes in Germany, Strads and all sorts. It's probably old, but not much good. And I don't know what to tell Tim. It's awful.'

'He keeps asking for Mischa,' said Madeleine.

The Inspector considered. 'You'd better tell him that there was a burglary here. Luckily his violin wasn't stolen. Mischa has gone unexpectedly to stay with friends for Christmas. How's that?'

'It's awful,' I said again. 'Not your idea, I mean. Mischa.'

'We won't have despair, Miss Firth.' He gave me the twinkling blue-eyed look. 'Don't give way to it. He may be hidden somewhere. He may be in hospital suffering from loss of memory. We keep checking. We're not going to give up, and nor must you.'

'I'm sorry.'

A new nightmare idea rose in my tired mind. Perhaps Mischa had gone to London Airport with someone else driving. Perhaps he had gone abroad. To get away.

I pushed the thought down.

'Tell Tim to look after it very, very carefully,' said the Inspector. 'It might be a good idea to show it to an expert. Just in case.'

We said goodnight. The Inspector put on his coat, then he woke up Grainger and told him to go home and get some sleep. Someone was coming to guard the studio for the night, and there was a squad car outside in the square. We were well protected, now, when it was too late.

We took the violin and went back through the cupboard and upstairs to bed.

'I'm sure I've forgotten something. Something I meant to tell him.'

'You told him everything,' said Madeleine. 'Gosh, you were good.'

'Why was he so nasty, about Sandy?'

'He wanted to see if you changed your mind or acted guilty when you heard she was dead. But you didn't. So he knew you were a solid character and that everything else you had said was true.'

'Funny way of finding out. I'm exhausted. Goodnight.'

'Goodnight.'

I put the violin under my desk, threw off my clothes and crawled into bed.

Deep sleep, oblivon. So tired.

Then suddenly some loud noise woke me and I jumped upright, heart beating fast. Telephone.

I scrambled out of bed. Mischa, telephoning. It must be. Everything all right. I tottered down to the next landing. Madeleine's door opened and she came down after me.

The ringing stopped. We stood on the stairs and looked at each other, bleary-eyed. I felt as if I'd only been asleep five minutes.

'Bobby must have answered,' I said. 'In the study.'

We went on down. The call was over before we'd reached the ground floor. We heard the bell ping on the living-room telephone.

Bobby came out of the study, dressed in hearty school-girl pyjamas.

'Lord.' Only the slightest tremor. She'd always had good nerves. 'We mustn't panic. Come in here. He's going to ring again.'

'Who, who?'

We sat on the couch. She told us. A man. He knew where

Mischa Lewis was. Safe. As well as could be expected. The man wanted money, a lot of money, and he'd tell where. Seventy-five thousand pounds. No police. The *Chronicle* could find the money. Bobby was to arrange it with the editor.

'Ring him,' I said. 'Ring him now. Please Bobby, please.'

'You'd better ring the police first,' said Madeleine.

'No! He said no police, didn't he Bobby –' I couldn't bear it. Mischa was alive. We only had to get the money. Bobby only had to lift the telephone.

'They always say that,' said Bobby. 'Lord, every kidnapper you ever hear of says don't call the police or else.'

'Or else! Bobby, how could you. It's Mischa, it's his life –'

'He was quite nice, that man,' said Bobby thoughtfully. 'He said he was on his own, he didn't want no trouble. Mischa was a first class batsman, he said. Lord, I don't know what the big white chief is going to say.'

She telephoned him. They spoke long and earnestly. He said the *Chronicle* would provide the ransom money. What a scoop! He'd get the crime desk on to it right away. Incidentally, wasn't Bobby due for a rise? Bobby said thank you, she'd take the rise. But could she handle the story herself? The big white chief said she could.

Then she rang Inspector Gregson. It was four in the morning. He came back, bright and cheerful. He sat with Bobby in the study. Madeleine went back to bed. I lay under my Irish rug on the living-room sofa. It wasn't comfortable and I couldn't sleep anyhow. I kept thinking about Mischa, wondering how he was.

As well as can be expected. Horrible. Horrible.

The telephone didn't ring again. I waited and waited. I made tea for the Inspector and Bobby. It was almost breakfast-time.

The beginning of another nightmare day.

*Once More from the
Double Bar*

I

'Nurse, where are you?'

Mischa propped himself on one elbow and looked round the cabin. Daylight. Raindrops were streaming past the porthole, and the boat was rocking unevenly. He could hear waves slapping at its sides and rain pattering down on the deck above his head. It must be windy today, and wet.

No sign of Nurse. Perhaps he was at the other end of the boat. Try again, louder.

'Nurse!' His ribs hurt slightly when he shouted. But there was no doubt that he felt much better today. Except for a strange dream, which lingered in his mind, he'd slept well. His head wasn't too bad. A little dizzy when he sat up. Leg all right as long as he didn't attempt to move it.

'Nurse!'

No answer.

Time was a bit confused in his mind. Was it yesterday when they talked about Bobby and the ransom? And had baked beans for lunch? Then Nurse had slept for an hour or two in the other bunk, snoring heavily. Later he'd got up, on duty again like the good old Nurse he was, looking after Mischa like a baby, feeding him, changing the dressing on his head. They'd had a tasty supper and a glass of tea with rum in it, which hadn't done his head any harm. Yesterday.

Some time very late, or very early, Nurse had gone and Mischa had dropped off to sleep again. He remembered Nurse saying good-bye, in the doorway with his torch.

'Sorry matey. Going in to bat. Leave you in the pavilion. I'll fix the score with Bobby and I'll come back. I promise I will, matey. Have to lock the door meanwhile, see what I mean.'

He'd gone.

Mischa lay down again. He was alone. He felt very sorry for himself. Ten o'clock already, by his watch. Why wasn't Nurse back? Had he decided it was all too dangerous? Had he changed his mind, scarpered, left Mischa on his own to die?

Was Nurse a rat?

That dream had certainly been fantastic. Perhaps it was the rum Nurse had given him. Everything muddled up, ridiculous, yet perfectly convincing at the time. He'd been playing the Elgar Concerto in Birmingham and Sir Edward Elgar himself had come up specially to listen to the rehearsal.

'That phrase was imperfect to say the least,' said the great composer, frowning as he stroked his silky white moustache. 'Can we have it again please, Mischa? Mr Mirmanov will have to wait.'

Mirmanov was conducting. It was horribly embarrassing. The orchestra sat there while Mischa tried to get the phrase right and the more he tried the worse it got.

Elgar glared at him.

'Hopeless! This boy is hopeless! Where are his parents?'

Mischa's foster parents shuffled forward. They looked sweet and old. They took him by the hand and led him away protesting.

'I want to play!' he shouted. 'Give me one more chance, Elgar!'

'Mind your manners, Mischa,' said his foster mother.

'All right, Sir Edward then!' yelled Mischa. 'I don't care what he's called, I just want to play his concerto!'

'I'm sorry,' boomed Elgar, his voice becoming night-marishly loud. 'It's hopeless, hopeless, hopeless!'

'Come away, Mischa,' said his foster father. 'Come home to the shop. I'll find you another instrument, a nice bassoon or a trumpet.'

'No, no! I want my violin!'

The dream got worse and worse. His violin was floating away from him, writhing and turning through the air with a life of its own, getting further and further away. His bow sped after it like an arrow, caught up with the violin, and started playing hideous strange nonsense. There was no calling them back. They whirled off into space and dis-appeared altogether, and their discordant music died away.

That was his dream, a dream of loss and failure.

He'd probably never live to play the Elgar in public. All that practising, the hours of work he'd spent on the score. *Here lies enshrined a soul in torment* – that's what Elgar had written at the beginning. Yes, Mischa knew what those dreadful words meant now. It was him, poor old Mischa. A soul in torment, and a body in torment too. Enshrined in a houseboat with a broken leg, dying of starvation. He'd never play the Mendelssohn again, nor the Beethoven. No Elgar, no Tchaikovsky, no Sibelius. No more concertos for Mischa.

Sadly he remembered the Beethoven sonatas too, and those long practice sessions with Mac. What a pianist that man was, a sturdy little Scot all made of music. They'd played so well in recitals, really understanding each other, perfectly in accord. Sometimes when they were practising Mac would smile with pleasure. 'Och laddie,' he would say. 'Let's have it again from the double bar, just for the fun of it.' The tough vigorous hands would ripple over the piano in perfect, balanced rhythm. Mischa could hear in his head those special passages, the *adagio* of the 'Kreutzer', where

Mac turned the beautiful trills so neatly, each variation exquisite, clear and sweet. And the opening phrase in Opus 96, the G major. First the violin, then Mac echoing it on the piano. And that splendid helter-skelter in the *finale*, the two of them as one. And the 'Spring' sonata, F major. The *presto*, with Mac syncopating like a demon, never faltering.

What a musician he was, what an accompanist.

Mischa lay there in despair, thinking these depressing thoughts. Then quite suddenly he remembered something which made him sit up again. Mac was a first-class pianist and also a composer. He'd written two sonatas already, for violin and piano, dedicated to Julian de Courcy. A good violinist, a little older than Mischa, his nearest rival. De Courcy had played Mac's No 1 in A Major at a Prom and it had been broadcast too. The No 2 he'd played at the Cheltenham Festival. There was another sonata on the way. Mischa had seen the first movement some months ago. Mac had said he might finish it by Christmas. He would like it to be Mischa's sonata. Sonata No 3 in D Major by John Mackintosh, played by Mischa Lewis.

But if Mischa wasn't available, if he'd perished in some damp cold houseboat, Julian de Courcy would play Sonata No 3.

With that thought light seemed to flood into Mischa's stupid bandaged head and he decided that no matter what happened he must get up. He must get up and out. A few hundred yards away was the world, a world full of music. He must get out there and play. Why, here it was ten o'clock and he was lying in bed like a cripple. True, he had a broken leg. Nurse had had to lug him around, a dead weight. But Nurse was efficient, a good casualty man. He'd tied the thing up, immobilized it, he said. It couldn't be all that bad. Cautiously he drew aside his concert overcoat and the blankets and inspected it. Padded and splinted. Comfortable. Only a dull ache. It hurt if he wiggled his toes. And if he tried to bend his knee.

Ouch! He winced. It was going to be difficult, but never mind. He had to get up.

He sat for a while, plotting. He'd need crutches. There was a chair within reach, beside him. Another in the lavatory. He'd go there first.'

He put on his concert overcoat for warmth. It was dirty and torn and there was blood on the collar. Left leg over the side of the bunk, socked foot on to the floor.

'Arrgh!' he groaned. 'Arrgh!'

Poor old Mischa. Can't get around any more. Trouble with his leg. Julian de Courcy is going to play Sonata No 3 by John Mackintosh, in the Festival Hall.

That did it. He braced himself for the next move. He pulled the chair towards him, grasped the back of it with his left hand, raised his right hand to the bunk above him. Pushing with his left, pulling with his right. Up we go. Arrgh!

Slowly, slowly, nothing sudden. He stiffened his right knee. It was agony. Och laddie, I see you're suffering. Yes, Mac, I certainly am. I don't think I can go on. Bear it, laddie, bear it. Och, it's a grand little sonata I'm writing for you. Up you come, laddie!

He was standing. He felt sick and dizzy. Sweat dampened his forehead. He leaned weakly against the wall, keeping his right foot off the floor, and took a big breath. Then he began to inch himself the length of the bunk, carefully round the end of it, reached the lavatory door, opened it and stumbled, one-legged, inside. He leaned over the basin for a long time.

Raising his head at last he looked in the mirror. Dimly he saw a pale face, dwarfed under a helmet of dirty bandage. An adhesive plaster on one cheek. Black-ringed eyes.

Dark in here. Electricity not connected. A little rust

coloured water in the taps. Outside, just visible through a corner of the tiny porthole, was a whole river full of water, whipped into choppy waves. The tarpaulin outside hung down and obscured the view. It flapped loosely in the wind. There would be boats out there, barges, people looking for him. He banged on the thick glass. No good of course. Try the ventilator. He stood underneath it and yelled as loud as he could.

'Help! Help!'

That wasn't going to be much good either, unless there was someone near enough to hear him. On a day like this, with rain and wind, his voice wouldn't carry far. And the shouting hurt his bruised ribs. He would have to ration it.

After breakfast he'd make a plan.

Things were easier with the two chairs. He still had to be pretty careful, especially as the weather was rough. He swayed dangerously as he hitched himself onwards, pausing under the ventilator in the middle of the cabin to cry 'Help!' once more. Waste of breath. He reached the door which led through to the fore part of the boat. Yes, Nurse had locked it. Probably bolted on the outside too. He leaned heavily on one chair and shook the handle. Hopeless. The door was solid thick wood. The screws of the hinges were on the other side. Without a crowbar he saw no way of opening it.

Hunger gnawed at his stomach. Think about the door later. He had to eat. Come on, laddie, how about some porridge?

The kitchen door wasn't locked. Good old Nurse. He wasn't such a bad fellow. Mischa edged his way in, one chair first, then himself, then the other chair. He stood in front of the stove.

A scruffy piece of cardboard was propped up against the blue kettle, with a message in untidy thick pencil, hard to read.

Glad you got so far matey. Hammer and chisel in locker.
Take your time while I go in to bat. Wish me luck.
P S Borrowed your gloves hope you don't mind.

Mischa looked at it for a long time. Good old Nurse. He'd
thought it all out. He wanted Mischa to live, to get back
into the world and play his violin. He'd patched him up and
left him to do the rest himself. If he'd gone on lying in bed,
well, that was his own funeral. But if he was willing to make
the effort Nurse was going to make things easier.

Mischa reached up into the locker and found the hammer
and chisel. Dear good kind Nurse. He rested a while, leaning
on the stove, then he moved cautiously round the galley,
looking in all the lockers, taking out everything that was
edible and putting it so that he could reach it easily. There
was half a tank of calor gas and a gallon, almost, of paraffin
for the stove. There was a full box of matches. Nurse had
filled a jug of water for him and put it in the sink where he
was bound to see it. It was a nasty colour, obviously genuine Thames water. But it would be all right if boiled.

Mischa lit the gas. With some musty oatmeal and a
sprinkling of caked salt he made himself a large helping of
porridge, which he ate with golden syrup. Not quite the
porridge Mac liked, but never mind. A cup of black tea to
follow. He wouldn't bother about washing up. There wasn't
enough water to spare.

Lighting the paraffin stove was the most difficult thing
he'd had to do so far. He had to get down on the floor. He
put the matches in his overcoat pocket. It was like a day's
journey, shifting his weight gradually downwards with the
help of the chairs, getting his left hip down first so that the
right leg rested on top. Lying propped on his left elbow,
lighting the match, getting the thing to work, the wick rather
shaggy and untidy making an uneven flame, part blue and

part yellow. Pushing the whole stove along the floor towards the door he was going to work on. Well, once he'd started he'd be warm enough. At the moment he was cold and shaky.

Back to the galley, snaking along the floor. He had to get up again to collect his tools. The long pull up, the painful jolts and falterings. Standing one-legged again between his two chairs, the hammer and chisel in his pocket. How about another cup of tea, Mischa? Do you good. He boiled the blue kettle again, drank, and felt better. Once he'd got through to the main cabin he might find some whisky, or a bottle of beer. Sandy's bar. Once he was there he'd only have one door to get through. He'd be practically free. Up a few steps unfortunately, but he would manage that somehow.

He remembered Sandy's friends, drinking coke and beer and eating pills.

He shouted 'Help' up the galley ventilator and went back again into the cabin, settled in front of the door on one of his chairs and rested his right leg on the other. It took a little while to find a comfortable position. Everything had to be done slowly. All right once he settled. He took out the hammer and chisel and started chipping away at the doorjamb, so that the whole lock would fall free. It was slow work and his hands were cold. He rather wished Nurse hadn't taken his gloves, not only because of the cold. He was afraid of hurting his hands. He wasn't used to using tools, not this sort. When other boys had been hammering and sawing, little Mischa had been playing his violin. Several times he missed the top of the chisel and hit his left thumb. The nail was turning dark red. This worried him more than all his other pains.

Och laddie, you're doing fine. Another hour or two, you'll be in the main cabin. It's a grand little sonata.

Mischa hummed and sang as he worked. His ribs didn't

hurt so much, sitting like this. He went right through the Elgar, playing it all in his mind, hearing the orchestra behind him, longing for his violin and real music. Then he did the Tchaikovsky. Dah, dah, dah, di-di dah, dah, dah. Beautiful, couldn't wait to get out and play it. Hammer hammer. Bang bang. Mind that thumb. Ouch.

He stopped to suck it. He'd drawn blood, gouging splinters of wood out of the door-frame. Nearly through. Looking up from his labours he realized that it was darker. It had been a dark day to begin with, and now, so soon, the afternoon was beginning to draw in. He looked at his watch. Amazingly it was three o'clock. He needed lunch. Better to down tools. No use hitting your fingers to pieces. Might need them later. He'd do the rest tomorrow.

Adjourn to the pavilion. Hearty meal of spaghetti, tinned apricots, and a handful of currants which had crystallized into a sugary black lump. Hot black tea. Painfully, happily, back to bed.

He turned the stove out on his way back. Could be dangerous. Rain still drumming on the tarpaulin above. The boat lying more peacefully as the wind dropped. He crawled under the covers, exhausted but triumphant. No matter what happened he would hammer and bang his way out tomorrow. If necessary, if hammer and chisel failed, he'd use his teeth. He'd gnaw his way out like a rat.

He smiled and thought of Nurse.

Bad light stopped play, Nurse. But I'll be back there tomorrow.

I'll get up early. Practising always best first thing in the morning. I'll tackle the Bach Partita again, that last section where the double stopping eases off and everything comes out clear. I'll play it right, everything perfect, every note, every tiny detail of phrasing.

Once more from the double bar, laddie.

2

Bobby sat in the study by the telephone all day. They were tapping it at the exchange. It rang constantly. Mischa's friends, his agent, and Mac, more furious than ever, rolling his r's and saying he had to speak to Mischa about a special pr-r-roject. And Boney's old man, all the way from Derby, wondering if he should come home. He got a good ticking-off for his trouble. Boney told him the telephone was needed for more urgent things and he should stay where he was. And friends of ours who'd seen the papers telephoned, wanting to know if we were all right. We said the same to all of them. There had been a burglary in the house next door, a gang apparently. They'd had a fight and left a dead body behind. Nothing to do with Mischa. They hadn't taken anything worth having. Mischa had gone away to stay with friends.

Had we seen in the papers, Sandy Lovelace murdered? My dear, how awful for Mischa. He must be very upset. They were practically engaged, weren't they? Well, that was all over a long time ago, we said. But Mischa was a bit upset. No, we didn't know where he was staying.

Over and over, the same conversation.

But the man who had telephoned Bobby about the ransom didn't call again. Bobby waited, dozing between calls, still sitting upright, her face grey with lack of sleep. Inspector Gregson said it might be a hoax, but we couldn't rule it out.

'It's because you called the police,' John told me. 'Vile idiot.'

'It wasn't me. It was Bobby.'

'She should have promised the money straight off and we'd have Mischa back by now.'

'Don't.'

Rain fell unceasingly. The wind blew. The remaining snow was battered and pitted with holes. It surrendered to the rain, melted and ran away with it, swirling along in the gutters. Everywhere was wet.

The Admiral came to the door. We took him in and told him everything. He was like one of the family, after all. And the doctor came, and we told him. He said he thought we should all get away as soon as Tim was better, anywhere, it didn't matter where, a hotel on the south coast or something like that. Madeleine said she'd telephone her mother and arrange everything. The château was huge, as big as a hotel on the south coast practically. We could take Bobby too, and Boney.

'Young Tim's responding,' said the doctor when he came downstairs. 'That's a bright spot on the horizon. He'll be sitting up and taking nourishment soon, Mrs Bowen. Give him anything he fancies. He must have lost a lot of weight.'

I remembered that I hadn't given Tim the violin. I consulted with Boney and she said it was almost lunch-time and he'd better have the violin afterwards. He was just getting well enough to be bored. He'd been in semi-darkness on account of the measles and couldn't look at books.

'We'll need a little shopping done too.' Boney looked pathetically at me. 'Would you, Charlotte dear? I don't feel quite myself today, I must admit. Oh dear. I can't believe it's us.'

I put on boots and a raincoat and struggled out into the wet. It was pelting. Geraldine and Fred stood at the corner under a big umbrella, talking to Mick. He had his coat collar turned up, hands in pockets. I didn't want to talk to them. I hurried past, holding the shopping-bag up to my face. I could get vegetables somewhere else.

'Hey, luv!' Mick beckoned.

Reluctantly I joined him under the barrow's projecting roof. The four of us huddled together like conspirators.

'Look,' he began. 'It's been a lot of trouble in your place. Cor. And we don't want to interfere –'

'All in the papers,' said Geraldine. 'That Sandy.'

'This copper came to the depot this morning,' said Fred. 'He ask me various questions and I answer straightforward. I'm used to it, see. Missing persons, all that lark, you ask the milkman. Well, you remember that day, when he was going away?'

'Who?'

'Your Mischa. And I say to you, does he want milk today? And you say No. He won't be back till tomorrow. Remember? Well, later that day I meet Sandy Lovelace, me and my darling here –' a nudge for Geraldine. 'And what happened?'

'She was sucking up to Fred, so sweet,' said Geraldine. 'My, you think she really loves him. How is he, and how's everything. And then she says –'

'Then,' interrupted Fred, 'she says she's just going round to see Mischa Lewis. Do I happen to know if he's at home? And I say, Beautiful, he's not there and he won't be back till tomorrow, not till lunch-time. Mind you, I didn't mention that to the copper. It slipped my mind, like.'

They all looked at me. Three pairs of eyes.

'Then today,' went on Fred, 'our Geraldine is coming down Angel Walk. Know where I mean? Behind the Judo Jim, there's a row of garages. She's walking along, this garage door is a little bitty open. And inside –'

'I remember this yellow van,' said Geraldine. 'It brought the crate on the afternoon of December twenty, near enough three-thirty, to number twenty-three, Nelson Square, during my hours of duty. In this garage just now I see the same identical Bedford van, and a man is spraying it blue. And that's definite.'

They were waiting for me to say something.

'Come on,' said Fred. 'We have a right to know what's going on, don't we? Once a friend, always a friend. Milk and eggs, day after day, all these years. When you were a little nipper, and John and Tim. And him next door, moving in. You remember?'

'Where is he then?' asked Mick.

I gave them the same old story.

'There was a burglary and they stole the violins which the Japanese was going to start a shop with, and there was a fight. Mr Yamaguchi got killed –'

'I saw him lying there,' confirmed Geraldine. 'My oh my.'

'And Sandy Lovelace was murdered but it's nothing to do with Mischa. He was a bit upset and he's gone to stay with friends.'

They looked at me in disbelief.

'Come on, luv. Tell us. Tell Mick the Barrer. And I'll tell you something else. You know the Garden. Covent Garden. I get my stuff there the past fifteen years, know it like the back of my hand. And I seen something. Nothing much, but I say to myself, Cor, that's it.'

'What?'

'Early this morning. Picking up my stuff. This little fella with a violin. Going in a caf. And I seen him before. I know the face. And I know he don't play the violin, never.'

He paused for effect.

'He come from the Karate Klub, King's Road.'

There. I'd known all along that Mr Lee was something to do with the whole dreadful business, right from the beginning.

'Did you tell the police?'

'No, luv. You don't want to go bothering them, they've got their work to do. He was round here just now, the plain-clothes. He asked the questions, I answered straight, like

Fred. You don't want to tell them things they don't ask you. You might get someone into trouble.'

'Mick, please, you've got it all wrong! Mischa didn't do anything, I tell you! And if we don't find him they might kill him too –'

I'd let the truth out, some of it.

'Sorry,' I mumbled on, while they gawped at me. 'It's all horrible. He's disappeared. I'm not meant to tell. Sorry.'

'You speak out, kid,' said Geraldine. 'We're all friends.'

I told them, incoherently, the agonizing facts. A man had telephoned to say he knew where Mischa was and that he was alive. He wanted money. The *Chronicle* had offered to pay. There had been no more news, no lead, nothing.

'Cor,' breathed Mick. 'Cor. It's kidnapping then.'

Raindrops pattered on the umbrella and dripped from the edge. We were all part of Nelson Square, like Mischa. Now we stood together, silent, heads down, sharing the misery of losing him.

'So why are we waiting?' said Geraldine suddenly. 'What we standing here for? Come on, we're going to see the Inspector, right now, and tell him the whole truth and nothing but.'

'I don't know about that, luv –' began Mick.

'Well, I better be getting along,' said Fred, almost at the same time.

'No you don't!' Geraldine's big eyes opened even wider than usual as she laid a hand firmly on his shoulder. 'Just you come along with me, cheeky. And you too, Mick. If there's anything we can do to help our Mischa we're going to do it, and that's definite. He's a musician, that man. He's worth ten of us, and we stand here doing nothing!'

Resistance collapsed. Meekly they followed her. Fred took the truck with him and parked it at the bottom of the square.

I took charge of Mick's barrow. They were gone a long time, and I had sold sprouts, potatoes, tangerines and a cabbage before they got back. They were glowing with pride. They'd got warm and dry in our kitchen. Boney had given them tea. They'd been one at a time into the studio and seen Inspector Gregson.

'My,' said Geraldine. 'He's definitely a fine man.'

'We'll find Mischa,' said Fred. 'You bet we will. Keep smiling.'

'Cor,' said Mick. 'A real gent. He didn't rough me up, nothing like that. He thanked me. Ta ever so, he says, and my information may lead to an arrest. Cor.'

3

We were clearing lunch. The Inspector sent for Boney. She was crying again when she came back.

They'd found someone they thought was the driver of the yellow Bedford van. He'd been stabbed in the back, in a telephone box in Wandsworth. He answered the description Boney had given Divisional C.I.D. the day before. Except for one item. When she said leather, did she mean fur? This had been found underneath the body.

It was one of Mischa's gloves.

A despair so deep, so painful. Bobby left the telephone. No good now. Once more we sat in the living-room, trying to face the fact that we would never see Mischa again. The friendly little narrow-faced man who had brought the crate into the studio was dead. He might have known where Mischa was. He couldn't tell anyone now.

Madeleine was wonderful to us. She sent Bobby to bed, to sleep, switched off the study telephone, and told her not to get up till supper-time. She took Boney into the kitchen, telling her she knew a recipe for a chocolate cake, French style, that was fun to do. She sent John and me up to see Tim, and said that when we came down we'd play bridge. She'd teach us. It sounded a dull game, but when we'd tried we'd see that it was the most fascinating of all things you could do with cards.

John had lost all hope. He stopped saying, 'We'll find him.' He said very little. He kept hanging on to me, like a small child, putting his arm round my shoulder and weighing me down.

'Oh please,' I said as we went upstairs together.' Must you.'

'I feel lonely,' he said, hanging even heavier.

I fetched the violin from my room. The case looked like a miniature coffin.

Tim was lying in bed with the radio on full-blast when we went in, obviously feeling much better. His face was still blotched with measles and he was weak and frequently tearful. But the worst was over. Madeleine had given him a fictional account of what had happened which seemed to cover any evidence he might have picked up for himself. Feeling better, he'd drawn his curtains back and had an occasional look into the square. There was a police car, sometimes two. Nipping out of bed and on to the landing, he'd seen a policeman downstairs, drinking a cup of tea and talking to Bobby.

'It's an exciting burglary, isn't it,' he remarked. 'Have they found the people? When is Mischa coming back? Not till after Christmas? Oh. How long are the policemen staying? What did the burglars take? Did they just take the Japanese violins and is the Japanese man cross? Did they take Mischa's tape-recorder? No, that's good. Was it in the papers? Can I see? Why not, why? I want to see the papers.'

He threatened to cry.

'Look Tim,' I said quickly. 'It's your violin. Wasn't it lucky they didn't take it. Let's have a look.'

He sat up and I laid it on his knee.

'Mmmm,' he said, pressing the one remaining catch. 'I'll have to mend the case up a bit. Or you can do it for me, John. Mmmm. Oooh.'

He lifted the embroidered silk cover and laid it gently on one side. He took the neck of the violin in his skinny little hands and raised it from its blue felt bed. He gazed at it with the deepest admiration.

'It's beautiful,' he murmured. 'So beautiful. It's too beautiful for me.'

'There's a label inside somewhere,' I said. 'Let me show you.'

'Careful!' he squeaked. 'You mustn't put your hands on the varnish! It's precious. Look, like this.'

Funny old Tim. He held the violin just as Mischa would, fingers clear of the murky brown belly. Even cleaned up I didn't think the varnish would be much good. But I didn't want to upset him. He gazed into the f-hole, twisting his head to try and read what was inside.

'Let me have a look,' said John. 'Oh. Tricky, isn't it. What a silly place to put a label. I'll get a torch. And my magnifying-glass.'

It all helped pass the time. The dreadful load of sadness seemed less when you had something to do. We spent fifteen minutes peering inside the violin, trying to decipher what was written on the discoloured piece of paper lying inside.

'JOF,' said Tim. 'It says JOF.'

'That's not an F, it's an old-fashioned S,' said John. 'You get them in Shakespeare. Fakes-fear, I mean. Actually they only come in the middle of a word. Look, this is what we've got so far.'

He wrote out what he could see, then I had a turn and added a bit more. Eventually we had the whole label. We read it out to Tim.

Joseph Guarnerius fecit ✠ Cremone anno 1740 IHS

'Fake-it?' Tim said in dismay. 'Does it say fake-it?'

'Stupid,' said John. 'That's Latin. *Fecit* means he made. Joseph Guarnerius made it in Cremona in the year 1740. Funny, the forty is written separately from the rest of the date, different pen. Actually I think it should be *Cremonae*. It should be in the locative case.'

'Should it?' Tim had another look. 'No, I think it's right like it is. Why does it have a little cross at the end?'

'I don't know. Perhaps he was rather holy. And that IHS, that's holy. You see it in churches.'

'Yes,' said Tim. 'I seen it sometimes. And the f-holes have a look of church too, see? Pointed at the top, rather narrow. Not like ordinary violins.'

He lifted it reverently and laid it back in its case.

'It's so beautiful I'm not going to play with it any more. I'm going to keep it shut until Mischa comes back. It can be my Christmas present for him, because he's always wanted a real one and here it is. He only needs to put some new strings and then he can play it in the Festival Hall.'

There was a short silence.

John got up suddenly and went out. I heard him go into

his own room and shut the door. I didn't know what to say. I stared fixedly at Tim's eiderdown.

'Why are you crying?' he said suspiciously.

'I'm not,' I sniffed. 'I might be getting a cold.'

He gave me a knowing look. 'It's that Graham.'

'Yes,' I said hurriedly, grateful for the excuse. 'It's Graham.'

'Hasn't he telephoned?'

'No. Oh Tim, I wish he would come back!'

'Poor old Charlotte,' he said kindly, patting me. 'He'll come back, I know he will. He'll be back for Christmas. Here, have my hanky.'

He tucked the violin in its case into bed with him, as if it were a teddy.

Rain fell all afternoon. Bobby got up and went home to fetch some clean clothes. She said she was going to stay with us. She couldn't bear to be somewhere else. Did we mind?

We wanted her to stay. We wanted friends, close friends, people who knew.

She telephoned the *Chronicle* and spoke to the big white chief again.

'Actually he's a big white bastard,' she said. 'Lord, he must be the meanest man on earth.'

'Why?'

'Yesterday he was offering seventy-five thousand for the ransom because it made a good story. Now its down to five thousand for news. It's not exclusive any more. The police have released details.'

We watched the news on television. Everything was there. Photographs of Sandy. Her car. Mischa holding a violin, with his hair brushed back smooth and plastered down. The telephone box in Wandsworth where a man, believed to be Mr Lewis's kidnapper, had been found dead. The *Chronicle* was offering five thousand pounds for news of Mr Lewis's whereabouts.

They went on and on. Indignation made us talkative again, and hopeful. We'd been right down at the bottom. Now we were climbing up again out of that same pit of despair. We'd find him. He must be somewhere. He was young and strong. Anything might have happened. Loss of memory, almost certainly. But he'd get over that. We'd find him.

We had supper, all talking, eager and hungry. The chocolate cake was a dream of deliciousness. Bobby cursed and swore at the editor of the *Chronicle* and we cursed and swore with her.

Afterwards we played bridge. It was fun. The telephone started ringing again and we took it in turns to answer so that someone else could join the bridge four. All Mischa's friends rang again. They'd heard the news. We'll find him, we said cheerfully. We mustn't give up. It's awful, but we mustn't give up. We'll find him.

4

Inspector Gregson came in from his headquarters in the studio at half-past eleven. John had gone to bed and so had Bobby and Boney.

Madeleine and I sat with him at the kitchen table.

'I'm sorry,' he said. 'I'm an owl, I hunt at night. I thought you might like to know that we've rounded up some of the culprits.'

He didn't look all that cheerful. The blue eyes had lost their sparkle. He was probably tired. Even owls get tired.

A lot had happened during the day, he told us, all sorts of things that the public would never know about. The police had been very busy, not only in London but all over the place. They'd caught up with Lee in New York, a passenger on a flight from Heathrow which had been much delayed by weather conditions. He had no luggage, only an airline bag bought at the airport, and he was travelling under a false name with a forged passport. They'd found two Japanese businessmen boarding a plane in Hawaii, Yamaguchi's friends. Checking on Lee's establishments up and down the King's Road they'd found three of the heroin-laden violins, another in a café in Covent Garden, and two last ones in a strip club in Soho. The whole represented one of the biggest drug hauls Scotland Yard had ever made.

'It was a ring,' explained the Inspector. 'Or rather two concentric rings. Lee had contacts on the Chinese mainland, where the heroin was produced. He heard about Yamaguchi's enterprise, and horned in. The stuff was packed in Japan and shipped to Europe. Beautifully done, sometimes in cars, sometimes in furniture. This lot in musical instruments. Only someone who knew it was there would be able to find it. They've been at it for some years. It was the clash of the two gangs which broke everything up. A few loose ends to tidy, and that's all.'

'And Mischa?' we asked.

The blue eyes drooped.

'I'm sorry,' he said. 'Lee and his friends seem to agree on this point. He was beaten up. They deputed someone to get rid of him. The man who demanded ransom, in fact. The River Police will be dragging Chelsea Reach tomorrow. Yes, it's unpleasant. But I still don't want despair, Miss Firth. It's routine. I had to tell you. They'll start just opposite Lot's

Passage. I should avoid that stretch tomorrow if I were you.'

'It's too horrible. I can't believe it.'

'Well, don't. I've been long enough in this business to know that life is full of surprises. We've searched the Judo Jim and the Karate Klub. Every inch of all Lee's property in the King's Road. But it turns out he had other investments all over London, garages, betting-shops, warehouses. We're working through them all one by one. We'll find him.'

We said goodnight.

I couldn't sleep.

We'll find him. But it would be too late. He would be dead, a silent body lying in a wooden box, like Tim's violin. A body brown with Thames mud.

We'll find him.

Rose

I

The twenty-third.

Waking up was the worst part, consciousness coming and bringing with it the knowledge that our lives were still horrible. I got up late, hardly rested, jumpy, bad-tempered. I really hadn't slept more than a couple of hours.

I quarrelled with John on my way downstairs. Tim shouted at me and burst into tears because I hadn't said good morning to his violin. The telephone rang incessantly, friends who hadn't rung before and the same ones who'd rung yesterday, all over again. I answered for an hour, then Bobby relieved me. Sightseers drifted in from their Christmas shopping in the King's Road to stare at the studio. The doorbell rang. Reporters tried to get into the house and had to be diverted by a constable lent specially by Inspector Gregson. We were besieged for the second time.

'I can't bear it,' said Boney. 'I'm going to do the laundry. The machine makes a nice lot of noise. It'll drown the other.'

'Come on, John,' said Madeleine. 'It's fine today. We'd better clean the motor-bike. We'll take it to the other end of the square.'

John brightened up. He collected a bucket of soapy water and two sponges and a bath towel which he pinched from the pile of dirty washing while Boney wasn't looking. Madeleine spotted it at once and made him put it back. They went down into Boney's basement together and came up the area steps to avoid the reporters who were lurking outside the studio.

It was a better day. The rain had washed the square clean and the wind had dropped. After a while I decided that fresh air would be good and I put on a coat and followed Madeleine and John. They were making a fine job of the bike. It was clean and sparkling. Mick admired it, and so did Geraldine and Fred. Since I'd confided in them, they were our friends far more than before. They knew how we felt. Tactfully they said nothing about the news which filled the papers and stared at us from the news-stand on the far side of the King's Road.

VIOLINIST BELIEVED HIDDEN.
KIDNAP MURDER MYSTERY.
ARRESTS IN CHELSEA DRUGS CASE.
HAVE YOU SEEN THIS MAN?

Photographs of Mischa on the front pages of the dailies, and in the *Chronicle* a huge spread about the reward they were offering. People, heavy with Christmas parcels, stopping to look at the square and point to the studio at the bottom. Yes, that's where he lived. They found that body there, the other day. They say he was on drugs. Someone told me. It was on telly.

We tried not to listen.

'You couldn't take me for a ride, could you?' asked John. 'Just round the block.'

'Not without a crash helmet,' said Madeleine. 'I've only got one.'

The Admiral and Skipper happened along, going out for a walk. Yes, he had a helmet, just the thing, left in the hall by his nephew. Good show. Dear Admiral, all kindness too, not mentioning Mischa and the horrors. He gave John his door-key and told him to help himself.

I left them putting the finishing touches to the bike and walked off down the King's Road, turned left at Martineau Street and made for the Embankment. I didn't want to see, and yet I couldn't keep away.

The tide was low. Police were walking about the small strip of bare mud, poking and probing with sticks and rakes. A small crowd gathered to watch, leaning over the stone coping. Mothers lifted their children. Two police launches were out in midstream, spreading some sort of net between them.

Disgusting.

I felt slightly sick. I turned quickly westwards and went fast, past Albert Bridge and on, not heading anywhere, just trying to get away. Disgusting. The thought of the body, the police pulling up something. Mischa's coat or a shoe.

I walked on, wretched and aimless. Battersea Bridge. The houseboats. It had been all cold and misty that day when we'd walked down here, Mischa and I, before my exam.

I paused, breathing fast from my walk. Now the river shone smooth and clear in wintry sunshine. The little blue boat with the mermaid prow lay out there beyond the barge, covered in tarpaulin. Horrible Sandy. Her fault, all of it. Misery and nightmare, drugs, robbery, violent death.

Our Mischa.

Like an aged relative visiting a grave I picked my way sorrowfully down the stone steps and over the walkway on to the damp deck of the barge. Somewhere in the Thames sludge a young violinist lay dead, battered, drowned. All his life's work gone for good, his music silent. No River Police could dredge that up.

They were mending something, out there at the end of the barge. Some happy person was hammering and whistling. The tune floated over the water like a trumpet call.

Someone was shouting at me.

'Charlotte, dear girl!' The Admiral waved frantically from the bank. 'Please don't do anything rash! Wait, I'm coming!'

'I'm all right!' I yelled back. Silly old Admiral. He probably thought I was going to commit suicide or something. The water couldn't be very deep here. A sensible suicide would have chosen the bridge. But then suicides aren't sensible anyway.

I turned and started walking back towards him. He was on the barge, urging Skipper to brave the narrow walkway and join him.

The hammering stopped. The little tune again.

I knew it. A tune for the violin, but a trumpet sort of tune.

Beethoven. The *rondo* of the violin concerto.

'Mischa!' My voice had gone hoarse. 'Mischa!'

I turned and started running back along the barge, the Admiral calling after me. 'Charlotte! Please, don't jump! Stop her, Skipper!'

I slipped and fell, got up in agony, and hobbled on, with Skipper barking loudly at my side.

'It's Mischa!' I cried, rubbing my knee. 'Ouch! I heard him, he's here!'

The Admiral caught me up and gripped me firmly by the arm. 'Steady, old girl. Good show. Nerves give way sometimes –'

He stopped. We both listened. Skipper waited, trembling. Uncertainly the Admiral raised his voice. 'Ahoy there!'

The answer seemed to come from underneath, from both sides, from the bank, from the middle of the river. Faint but distinct.

'Get me out of here before I ruin my hands!'

Our Mischa.

Skipper gave a bark of triumph, ran to the end of the

barge, jumped aboard the blue boat with the mermaid prow and disappeared under the tarpaulin.

I don't know what happened next. Time went very slowly. We followed Skipper, like snails. Everything seemed agonizing, leisurely, a new variation of the nightmare. Under the tarpaulin, in darkness. Skipper barking and scratching. The door locked. Mischa calling to us, alive and well. There were two locked doors. We'd need a crowbar.

I think the Admiral went for help. I shouted to Mischa and he shouted back. Skipper scratched and yelped. There was a fire-engine and blue revolving lights and an ambulance and a police-car, when I put my head outside the tarpaulin to look. People were crowding to the edge of the Embankment. Madeleine was there and John, on the back of the bike, wearing a gold crash helmet. Fred's truck was there and so was Fred, and Geraldine, and Mick and his barrow. The firemen got the doors open and fetched Mischa out on a stretcher. He kept on sitting up and trying to get off. He said he could walk if Nurse helped him. He was dirty and unshaven. His concert overcoat was torn and bloodstained. There was a tattered bandage on his head. His right leg was tied between bits of wood. His face was pale, his eyes huge and black.

We walked modestly behind the stretcher, the Admiral, Skipper and I. The firemen helped us ashore as if we were royalty. We bowed to the crowd. We waved. We nodded to our friends.

'Hallo Mischa,' said John in a shaky voice.

'Hallo John,' said Mischa from his lying-down position. 'How's Tim?'

'Fine.'

'Gosh,' said Madeleine. 'Gosh. You found him.'

'No, I didn't.' I pointed to Skipper. 'He did. He's just won five thousand pounds.'

Skipper wagged his tail.

They put Mischa in the ambulance.

'I'm his sister,' I said, and got in too.

'So am I,' said Madeleine. She handed her helmet to the Admiral. 'Could you take the bike home for me please?'

The crowd stood there on the Embankment goggling at us. The ambulance men closed the doors. The sirens started up. We sped through the streets with the police-car behind us.

'Who are you?' said Mischa.

'I'm Madeleine,' said Madeleine. 'I'm a doctor. At least I'm nearly a doctor. I'm a medical student.'

'Doctor,' said Mischa. 'You don't happen to know what happened to Nurse, do you? I'm terribly afraid they must have bowled him first ball.'

Madeleine looked at me significantly.

'Delirious,' she said.

'Nurse fixed my leg, Doctor. I'm not worried about that. It's this thumbnail. And a cut on this finger, look. I did it with a chisel, Doctor.'

'There, there,' said Madeleine. 'They're often like this,' she confided. 'A man came into hospital the other day, he was a fisherman off a trawler which had been wrecked in the North Sea —'

'Your hair would make a lovely violin bow, Doctor. I'd get a nice ginger tone, with a bit of golden syrup —'

She took his pulse.

'Aimez-vous Brahms?' Mischa asked her.

'Yes. I like the sonatas, especially No 3. Don't talk too much. It's better to rest.'

'I thought you were French.'

'I'm half and half.'

'What about modern music, Tippett and Britten, do you like that sort of thing, Doctor? And John Mackintosh?'

'Yes, I do. Don't worry about it now.'

The ambulance turned into the hospital courtyard. Most of the staff seemed to be waiting for us on the steps. They rushed Mischa inside. They examined him and prodded him all over. They X-rayed his leg and put it in plaster. They shaved his hair off down the middle and put two stitches in his head. They washed him and fussed over him and gave him a cup of tea and glucose and a sedative. They tucked him up in a clean white bed. A policeman sat by his side with a pad and pencil, waiting for him to wake up again.

Matron herself came to Mischa's room. She was a big angular Scot, rather fierce. She melted when she saw him. We stood with her, Madeleine and I, and gazed at him like mothers admiring a beautiful baby asleep in its pram.

'He's not usually so pale,' I apologized.

'Long eyelashes,' said Madeleine.

'Poor wee laddie,' said Matron. Mischa smiled in his sleep.

We were just leaving when we saw a familiar figure trying to creep into Mischa's room. It was John Mackintosh.

'Och, no you don't!' said Matron firmly. 'No visitors until this evening, thank you very much.'

Guilty but unabashed, Mac held out a large brown envelope.

'Forgive me, fair lady,' he said, exaggerating his Glasgow accent. 'You wouldna turn away a fellow countryman? Wi' a wee package of gr-r-r-eat importance?'

'Och weel –' Matron hesitated. 'He's asleep the noo. What would ye have inside?'

Mac explained. It was his sonata. He'd just finished it. Could he leave it so that Mischa would see it as soon as he woke?

'You'll understand, Matron. It's a true Scottish composition, entitled Sonata No 3 in G Major, by John Mackintosh. Sub-title The Isle of Lewis. It's a joke, ye ken, his name being Lewis.'

'The Isle of Lewis! Och, Stornoway is where I was borr-r-n!'

Mac laid the sonata on Mischa's bedside table.

'Och laddie,' he said. 'And I thought I'd have to find another violinist!'

We went downstairs. The great consultant who had put the plaster on Mischa's leg was in the X-ray room, holding up a damp grey negative. His students in their white coats grouped themselves behind him like a choir of angels.

'Gather round, gentlemen,' he said in his god-like voice. 'Observe that this simple fracture of the tibia was set by an unqualified thug, a villainous blood-letting gangster. If any of you ever set a broken bone as well as this I shall be very much surprised. If the genius who did this had not met an untimely end I would have been proud to invite him to give you a demonstration. Gentlemen, the world of medicine is the poorer for his demise.'

The angels sang his praises.

2

We went home in a taxi. It was four in the afternoon. We were tired and hungry and triumphant.

The square was full of people. There were reporters, television cameras and a policeman on a white horse. Geraldine,

Fred, Mick, the Admiral and Skipper were all there. Tim was leaning out of the window. John and Boney were standing on the doorstep. She was crying again.

'Oh dear. I can't believe it. Oh dear. What a Christmas we're going to have!'

'I hope it's goose,' said John.

'What's happening?' cried Tim. He'd left the window and was pattering downstairs in bare feet. 'Tell me, tell me!'

I took him upstairs, put him back in bed, and told him. It took a long time. Madeleine brought me a cup of coffee and a delicious sandwich. I ate and talked and Tim listened goggle-eyed.

'True? Not joking?'

'Not joking.' I'd left out Sandy. Perhaps later we could say something. That she'd died in a car crash. In a Florentine Gold Mini.

'So was my dream true?'

'I'm not sure. You were very ill and dreams are funny.'

'Yes. I dreamed the man said scarper, so I did.' He patted the violin case at his side. 'Won't Mischa be glad when he sees this!'

'I'll fetch you some tea, Tim. Are you hungry?'

'Yes, I am. I'm still a bit spotty but I'm better. And I tell you something, Charlotte.' His voice sunk to a horrified whisper. '*He might of died.*'

'I know, Tim. Too awful. Too awful to think about.'

'Mrs Kawate ray down and die.' He smiled, remembering. 'But Mischa Rewis riv for ever. I hope.'

'So do I, Tim.'

All afternoon the telephone rang and rang. Everything was different now. We rushed to answer it, falling over each other to get there first and tell the glad news. People wanted to come and interview me, but I said No. The *Chronicle* had scooped me. Bobby sat in the study outlining her story. She was going to see Mischa at visiting-time, and so was Boney.

Telegrams started to arrive, more and more. John and I sat on the living-room floor and opened them and sorted them into piles. Boney was in the kitchen with Madeleine, making a pie.

'It is going to be goose for Christmas,' said John. 'The Admiral says he'll come, and Bobby.'

'Let's have Mac too,' I said.

We thought of several other friends of Mischa's we'd like to have. When the telephone wasn't busy we rang them up and asked them for Christmas dinner.

'The more the merrier,' said Boney. The tears had dried up. She was singing as she plunged her big pink hands into the mixing-bowl.

Another call from the *Chronicle*. It was the editor, to congratulate me. I said it was Skipper really. I didn't know what to do with the money.

The doorbell, and another batch of telegrams.

'This one's for you,' said John, opening an envelope.

I snatched it from him and dashed out of the room, up the stairs.

'Hey, what's the matter?' he shouted after me.

I went into the parents' empty bedroom, shut the door behind me and put on the light. I spread out the crumpled message. I read it. My face went hot, burning hot. I read it again. Gasping for air, I went to the window, threw it open and leaned out. I took a big breath, cold and sweet like champagne, and gazed down into the square.

They'd given me a scholarship.

Down there under the street lamp was a familiar figure, looking sad and lonely.

'Graham!' I shouted.

He looked up and so did the reporters and photographers waiting patiently round our front door.

'Char! Are you all right? I've been trying to telephone –'

'I'm fine! They've given me a scholarship!'

I tore downstairs again waving the telegram. Graham met me at the door. The cameras caught us grinning and hugging each other. The reporters asked questions and Graham, usually so silent, said all the right things. I hardly had to bother.

'She deserved it,' he finished up. 'She worked very hard.'

We went inside. He rang home and said he wouldn't be in for supper. It was lovely to have him back. He didn't say much, but that's Graham. He spent a long time looking at the railway guide, trying to work out how to get to Cambridge from Leeds. In the end we decided that we'd have to meet somewhere halfway. But that wouldn't be until next autumn anyhow.

Inspector Gregson came later on.

'Congratulations,' he said. 'Twice over. I always suspected you were rather bright. The River Police are furious incidentally. You beat them to it. The houseboat was the next place on their list.'

'They should have looked there before they started dragging the river. Ugh.' The thought brought the nightmare back for a moment. 'Have you seen Mischa?'

'Yes. He made a statement, and we had a long and satisfactory talk. Nice chap, isn't he. He's had a thoroughly nasty experience, but bears no grudge. Quite upset to hear his kidnapper had been murdered.'

'Who did it, do you know? Was it the gang?'

'We believe so. This man was the weakling, the one at the bottom who always did what he was told. So when he disappeared Lee's men must have been suspicious. What was he up to? Was he informing the police? They spotted him going into a telephone box in Wandsworth, and that was the end. Nasty cold-blooded lot, Miss Firth.'

'Yes. They said he was good, at the hospital. He knew how to set bones.'

'So it seems. Mischa insists the little fellow saved his life. Says he would have stood up in the witness-box for him. Well, I'd better tidy up his studio and move back to the Yard. He'll probably be home for Christmas. If I may say so, it's been a pleasure working with you on the case.'

'Thanks. I never thought a detective would be like you.'

Blue eyes twinkled.

'We're full of surprises,' he said. 'You're looking after that violin, I hope? Good. Not a bad little instrument. Goodnight, and a happy Christmas.'

3

Christmas Eve.

Bobby's story came out in the *Chronicle*. It was thrilling, wonderful, terrifying. The big white chief was amazed. Perhaps she should do more reporting. But Bobby said Lord, no thank you, it was too exhausting.

People read all about us, and then let us sink back into obscurity. After that we weren't in the newspapers any more, nor on television. Other excitements pushed us out of the headlines, wars in the Middle East, typhoons in the West Indies, oil rigs in distress battered by heavy winter seas. The crowds deserted Nelson Square and went further down the King's Road, where a bank had been robbed. The whole front was made of glass and the gang had shot it to pieces getting away. The street was covered with glittering crystal splinters. It was very spectacular.

We were no longer news.

The shops were closed and all the bustle and buying of Christmas was over. For anyone who had not bought enough presents it was mercifully too late. Tomorrow would be Christmas Day, all peace and rejoicing.

A little evening mist lay over Nelson Square when Mischa came home. The street lamps shone pale gold on the few loyal fans who still waited outside his door. They clapped when the ambulance stopped and Mischa hobbled out into the cool night air, dragging his big plaster leg. The remains of his hair sprouted below the bandage on his head. He was well and smiling, glad to be back.

Carol singers raised their small voices. While shepherds washed their socks by night. Neighbours opened their windows and waved. Lights twinkled on miniature Christmas trees framed in tall windows. Glory shone around.

'Mischa, Mischa, Mischa!' shouted Tim from the landing.

'Back to bed,' said Boney. 'You can see him properly in the morning.'

'Gosh,' said Madeleine. 'You look better than last time.'

'Hallo, Mischa,' said John.

'Lord,' said Bobby.

'Good show,' said the Admiral.

Skipper wagged his tail.

The studio was clean and tidy and full of flowers. We'd arranged everything specially for our invalid. The telegrams and letters which had poured in were laid out in neat rows. The bed was in the middle of the room, and the sofa nearby, and the tape-recorder and record-player where he could reach them. We led him in and settled him on the sofa with a rug over his knees. The plaster cast bulged. We brought him a glass of white wine and a delicious supper, leaving the broom-cupboard door open so that he could see us in the distance and not feel lonely. We visited him one at a time and spoke quietly.

We were very happy and so was he. He fell asleep on the sofa with Mac's sonata in his hands. Madeleine and I had to wake him to get him into bed. We tucked him up.

We were very busy, making surprises and wrapping presents and stuffing the goose and decorating the exotic pudding which Madeleine had made for the feast next day. We put the tree Mick had given us in the living-room and covered it with beautiful shiny globes and stars and dripping tinsel. We arranged the presents all round it.

'I don't know what I would have done with this,' said John, wrapping the violin-shaped ashtray he'd made for Mischa. 'It wouldn't have suited anyone else.'

Later he crept into Tim's room with a heavily laden sock to replace the empty one drooping from the end of the bed.

'It's funny,' he said. 'I think I've grown up. I'm Father Christmas, because Alan isn't here.'

'You'd better go to bed now,' said Boney. 'Or you'll be Father Too-tired in the morning.'

4

Christmas Day.

A beautiful quiet all over London, peace and goodwill, cold white mist softening the cornices and balconies and rooftops in the square. John and Boney went to church and the vicar thanked God for Mischa's safe return. Tim unpacked his Christmas sock and spread the contents, including a chocolate Father Christmas and a lot of small sweets, all over his bed. Then he sneaked down to the living-room when nobody was looking and opened a few presents at random, muddling the labels so that we didn't know who had given what. The doctor came, in an old tweed suit with a piece of holly in his buttonhole, and had to admit his patient was recovering rapidly.

'Can I go and see Mischa then, please, please, please?'

'Well, just for a few minutes, Tim old boy. He's tired, you know. And then straight back to bed. No more running about with bare feet.'

'All right. It's just to give him his present.'

We wrapped Tim and the violin in an eiderdown and took them down to the studio. We settled him on Mischa's bed. Mischa sat on the sofa, surrounded by pillows and presents and letters and telegrams. My present, the black silk scarf, was draped elegantly round his head to hide the bandage. He looked like an oriental prince.

'Hallo Tim. How's the measles?'

'Nearly better, thank you. I like your hat.'

'It's the latest fashion,' said Mischa. 'And this is my new winter boot. It's very heavy, so I only wear one.'

He held out his right leg for Tim's inspection. Tim fingered the plaster and shook his head.

'It's a bit awful,' he said. 'I'll be gladder when it's off.'

Mischa covered it up with the rug and gave Tim a small parcel.

'This is for you, Tim. Happy Christmas.'

It was an alarm clock, a good one, with a luminous dial. Tim was very pleased. It was a proper present, very grown-up.

'And this is for you, Mischa. Happy Christmas.'

He pushed the violin case along the eiderdown.

'Thank you, Tim. It's very nice of you. I really meant you to have it. Let's have a look.'

We left them to it. We were going to have a small cold lunch, in the kitchen. The big feast was to be at seven in the evening. The goose was ready for the oven. Potatoes were peeled. Sauces nestled in small pans waiting to be heated at the last moment. I went into the dining-room with Madeleine to lay the table. There were going to be twelve of us. We had to add an extension and we couldn't get it to fit and John had to come and help. Then we had to get out extra silver and a long table-cloth and candlesticks and candles. We called for John again to collect chairs from the bedrooms.

'Busy!' he shouted from the studio. 'I'm helping Mischa!'

I fetched the chairs myself. On the way downstairs I saw John in the broom cupboard, pondering over a handful of dusters.

'What are you after?' said Boney.

'A soft cloth,' said John. 'Please Boney. It's for the violin. Not an old sock, that's too hairy. A really soft one.'

'Here, take this then. And keep out of my way, there's a good boy. A goose doesn't cook itself, you know.'

I looked through into the studio next time I passed. Mischa was re-stringing the violin and John and Tim were watching intently.

'Boys are extraordinary,' I said to Madeleine in the dining-room. 'They start on some ridiculous ploy just when you want them to help. They can't see what's important.'

'No sense of priorities,' agreed Madeleine. 'What about glasses, are these too precious?'

She paused with an engraved crystal wine glass balanced in her small fingers. Violin music began to drift through from the studio, first a slow sustained scale, then arpeggios, trills, wonderful arabesques of sound which swept from low broad growls to the thinnest and purest of high notes. She put her head on one side and listened.

'Gosh, it's got an unusual tone –'

'You can come!' called John suddenly. 'Everyone come, it's a surprise!'

We went into the studio. John, Mischa and Tim smiled mysteriously.

'Oh Mischa,' said Boney, 'that's your linseed oil on Tim's eiderdown. I don't call that much of a surprise. Really, you're more trouble than the lot of them.'

'Sorry, Boney. My hand slipped. I just can't believe it. I think it's a real one, a real Guarnerius. I'll play you some Bach, Boney. Just listen!'

He took up the violin again and bent his head over it, pausing a moment as if listening to a secret voice inside it. Then he lifted his bow and played the last section of the partita he'd been practising all that long time ago, before the snow and the terrible midwinter. He played as if he'd never been away, as if he'd just stopped to think for a few minutes and was now going on. The violin was strange to him, and he was weak, and out of practice by his standards. But all the same he made a strong vibrating noise which filled the studio, at first a struggling mass of notes and inter-locking phrases as the fugue reached its height, and then at last the triumphant logical conclusion, the answer to every-thing, the end of all troubles, the peaceful opposite to vio-lence. He seemed to forget his broken leg and his aches and pains and bruises. The music healed them, explained them away, made us all whole again. And when it stopped the place felt clean and empty.

Mischa put the instrument down and gently nodded his bandaged head.

'Yes, that's it,' he murmured. 'That's it.'

'It's super,' said John.

'It's genuine,' said Madeleine.

'Genuine,' I echoed.

'Lovely, Mischa,' said Boney. 'Gwarny whatever you say, it's lovely. Though I don't know what's wrong with your old one. A lot of fuss if you ask me. I'll get on with lunch.'

Mrs Kawate's violin, all dust smoothed away, lay sedately on the bed, glowing a luscious chestnut brown. Mischa kept looking at it, touching it here and there, pointing out to us the narrow upright f-holes and the fine texture of the pine belly. Then he turned it over so that we could admire the wavy grain of the maple back, which rippled like water in sunlight.

'It's a wonderful present, Tim. Wonderful. I never thought I'd be lucky enough to have one as good as this. Thank you very much.'

'I thought it was good,' said Tim generously. 'It had a look of goodness. And now I've heard it I know it's good. It gives you a funny feeling in your back teeth.'

'You're right,' said Mischa. 'Strads are different. You hear them in the nose. I've always preferred Guarnerius tone.'

'Will you play it in the Festival Hall?' asked Tim, winding up his clock and pressing and pulling the knobs on the back.

'Well, I'll see what it's like when I've played it more –' began Mischa.

The alarm suddenly went off and Tim jumped and we all laughed.

'Aha!' he cried. 'I got it, I see how it works! You play your violin in the Festival Hall, Mischa, and I'll play my clock! Thank you very much and a happy Christmas!'

We carried him upstairs to bed again, ringing all the way.

Mischa telephoned people while he ate his lunch. There

was an air of restrained excitement in the house. People telephoned him back. Mac came and disappeared into the studio. They closed the cupboard door. A taxi drew up outside and let out a very old white-haired man with a black bag. A famous violinist arrived in a chauffeur-driven Mercedes. And several other people. It was Christmas Day, but they came, springing out of their cars, leaping up Mischa's front steps, ringing his front doorbell loud and clear, eager to get in and see the mysterious violin. They were experts. They looked, they approved, they marvelled. They said it was certainly a genuine Guarnerius, the work of the last and greatest of that family of violin makers, Joseph or Giuseppe, who was known as Del Gesù, who died in 1744.

All great violins have a name. Mischa called his the Rose of Japan, after his friend Mrs Rose Kawate. It took its place with Del Gesù's other famous instruments, the Plowden, the Lafont, the Ex-Vieuxtemps, the Gibson, the De Bériot which was used for the first performance of Tchaikovsky's violin concerto, and Paganini's own Guarnerius. The experts said the Rose must have left Italy and gone to Russia at the end of the eighteenth century, when Italian violins were much sought after. From Russia it had gone to Japan, during the Revolution. The Kawate family had had it for a generation, lying unused. From Japan it had come to Mischa.

The long voyage was over.

In the afternoon, while the goose sizzled in the oven, we sat round the Christmas tree and opened presents, beautiful books and boxes of chocolates and crystallized fruits and toys and games and clothes, more presents than we had ever had before. People we didn't even know had sent us things. We arranged them all round the room.

Our guests arrived. Boney, dressed in pink with a butterfly brooch given by Tim, received them. Graham was the first, and brought me a football sweater. 'We all wear them in Leeds,' he said. I had my Christmas dress on, and I think he liked it. Madeleine was in black velvet. John wore a new pair of jeans and a new shirt and an amazing tie. Mischa and Tim wore pyjamas and ate quietly in their beds.

The meal was delicious and unusual and very, very filling.

'If I may,' said the Admiral, rising to his feet with an effort, 'I'd like to propose a toast. To Charlotte. Jolly good show.'

Then I proposed Boney, who'd cooked the dinner, and Boney proposed Madeleine, who'd given the wine. We drank everybody's health. We drank to Mac's sonata and Mischa and Bobby's story and John and Tim and Graham and the Guarnerius violin. We drank to Skipper. He wagged his tail and strolled off to join Mischa in the studio. The party was a bit noisy for him.

5

Boxing Day.

On a lonely coral island off the Great Barrier Reef the parents tuned their radio to receive the routine broadcast from the *Australian Princess.*

'And here is a message from Nelson Square, Chelsea. Tim had measles so we didn't go to France. Madeleine came to us instead on a bike. Charlotte has a scholarship and Leeds United won. Bobby wrote a story and the big white chief gave her a rise. Mischa has a broken leg and a Guarnerius. Skipper won five thousand pounds in a *Chronicle* competition. He has given five hundred to the Battersea Dogs' Home and five hundred each to Fred and Geraldine and Mick and the three of us will share the rest. We had a wonderful Christmas. John chose goose. Hope you are well. We are. Message ends.'

'Poor old Tim,' said my mother.

'I shouldn't worry,' said Alan. 'One gathers they've had a good time. Did it say something about a scholarship for Charlotte?'

'I think so. Perhaps it was all nonsense.'

'Funny sense of humour children have,' said Alan.

They walked down to the beach to continue their count of migrating crabs.

On Madeleine's last night we were invited to the studio for a performance of Mac's sonata. 'Just a run through, you understand,' he said. In fact they'd been practising for days.

'And make allowances for Rosie,' said Mischa. 'Playing her in. And sit well back. She's a loud-voiced old thing.'

Graham was there, and Madeleine and John and I. We arranged our chairs in a row in semi-darkness at the far end of the studio. Light shone on Mac and the piano and Mischa and his violin and his big white plaster cast. The sonata was full of the sound of the sea, just like the Isle of Lewis. The Guarnerius swooped and sang like a wild seabird.

'I like it,' said Graham, launching into one of his rare pronouncements. 'It has an abstract quality. It is intellectual and completely lacking in gimmickry, using the full potential of classical form. I like the way the second subject comes in with a fugal effect, overlapping the first, and the transition to the minor for the *adagio* is subtle, and then the *scherzo* is unusual because it's cerebral, not stupid the way they sometimes are. Based on a reel, isn't it. Do you think they'd play the *scherzo* again, just the last repeat?'

'Ask them.'

Mac was pleased. 'All right laddie, just once more from the double bar.'

Afterwards he asked Graham where he was studying music. Was it the Academy?

'No, Leeds,' said Graham. 'Chemistry.'

He's like that. When he's said what he wants to say he clams up. I think that's why I like him really.

'Goodbye Mischa,' said Madeleine.

'Goodbye Doctor. You will write, won't you. And you will come to my concert in February.'

John heard them. He was in the broom cupboard cleaning his shoes, and the door into the studio was open.

'He kissed her,' he told me afterwards. 'I know he did.'

'You're horrible,' I said. 'Eavesdropping like that. You should have made a noise so that they knew you were there.'

'I did, I made a vile racket. I stood up and hit the shelf and the big tin of polish fell on me. Look, there's a lump on my head.'

'Serve you right.'

February.

'I don't see our Mischa anywhere,' said Boney as the first and second violins filed into their places.

'Oh Boney, he doesn't come yet. He's the soloist, you see, he's special. They've got to play a boring old symphony first. Look, here's the programme.'

We had two boxes in the Festival Hall. Everyone was there, Tim and Boney and Bobby and the Admiral. John had a night off from school and Madeleine came down specially from Edinburgh and Graham from Leeds. And Geraldine was there, looking beautiful in a long dress, and Fred in a smart dark suit. And the parents were back, lean and tanned after nearly three months on the Great Barrier Reef. They'd had a most successful trip. The next book, *Coral Strands*, promised to be one of the best they'd ever done.

Boney's old man a.d Mick the Barrow had decided not to come to the concert. They said they'd spend the evening drinking Mischa's health at the Chelsea Arms instead.

Mischa got two standing ovations that night. He played the Tchaikovsky Concerto, and Sonata in D Major, No 3, by John Mackintosh, with the composer at the piano.

As we were leaving someone tapped me on the shoulder.

'Miss Firth!'

I turned round. Blue-eyed Inspector Gregson. He introduced his wife. We asked them to come with us and see Mischa in his dressing-room, but they had to rush to catch the last train home.

'I told you, didn't I,' said the Inspector. 'It's not a bad little instrument. Del Gesù.'

I remembered the night in the studio when he'd opened the battered old case and shown us the Rose of Japan, dusty with fingerprint powder, silent, asleep, unrecognized.

'Did you know all the time?' I asked.

'That it was genuine? Yes, I was pretty sure.'

'But how? It looked so ordinary.'

'Well, I'm a bit of a violinist myself. I've got a fake Guarnerius at home. Yes, you'd see the difference at once. I'll bring it round one day and show you.'

'You policemen are full of surprises.'

'Yes, I suppose we are. Goodnight!'

We hope you have enjoyed this book.
Some other adventure stories are
described on the following pages,
and there are 800 other Puffins to
choose from.

Mike and Me

David Line

Remember Jim Woolcott, who had terrifying adventures in *Run for Your Life* (on television, and in Puffins)? Well, here he is again, this time with his cousin Mike.

It all began when their art master began looking around for old books and documents for an exhibition about the history of the town and the school, and by discovering one particular old paper trod right on the toes of a bunch of greedy, ruthless speculators who wanted to make themselves a fortune. This is a must for any one who likes books with action and plenty of it.

The Eighteenth Emergency

Betsy Byars

Benjie and his friend Ezzie had spent a lot of time working out quick solutions to all sorts of emergencies, for instance Emergency 1: Lie down when sinking in a quicksand, Emergency 4: prop a stick in a crocodile's mouth to prevent it biting, and Emergency 11: If attacked by a werewolf, draw a six-pointed star and get inside it.

But there didn't seem to be a solution to an emergency like a hammering from Hammerman, the biggest, fiercest boy in the school – unless he counted the one idea that drifted into his head, like maybe even going to look for Hammerman when he wanted to hide from him. Could *that* be the golden key, the answer to the Eighteenth Emergency, the greatest one of all?

What About Me?

Gertie Evenhuis

Four years of war – blackout, gunfire, threadbare clothes and harsh German voices blaring through the streets, voices that sounded frightening even when they sang – in that time Dirk had grown into a serious eleven year old who desperately wanted to have a share in the secret goings-on of his elder brother, to *do* something to push the German invaders out of their lovely Amsterdam.

But when he saw the deadly result of his actions he knew that the fear of the Germans he had felt before was just a shadow of the terror he was feeling now – for his brother, for himself, and above all for the teacher whose life he had put in such peril.

The Partisan

Simon Watson

Dom was the Lord of the Circle of Boys, and Will was happy to obey the oath of allegiance he had sworn on the partisan. But when Will was left in charge and had to face the challenge of an older, brutal boy, and had to bear his own failure to keep the Circle intact, he realised how brave and responsible a leader must be.

If you have enjoyed reading this book and would like to know about others which we publish, why not join the Puffin Club? You will be sent the club magazine, *Puffin Post*, four times a year and a smart badge and membership book. You will also be able to enter all the competitions. For details of cost and an application form, send a stamped addressed envelope to:

The Puffin Club Dept A
Penguin Books Limited
Bath Road
Harmondsworth
Middlesex